HOOSIER NOIR

Hoosier NOIR

ONE

The follow is a collection of fiction. All names, places, and events in these stories are products not true. Any resemblance of any actual person (living, dead, or living dead), are strictly coincidental.

Front & back covers photos by Michael Mullen.

Cover and Interior layout by N E Riggs.

All book and magazine images via Amazon.

FirstCityBooks.com/HoosierNoir

HOOSIER noun

1. A native or inhabitant of Indiana.

2. An awkward, unsophisticated person.

Hoosier NOIR

Contents

Dunn & Dunn by J. Travis Grundon 9

Interrogating Rex Weiner 13

Author Spotlight: Alec Cizak 23

    Last Exit Before Toll 25

    Destroyers...29

Descent by Preston Lang 37

The Iceman by Les Edgerton...49

The Haunted Crave Knowing by J. Rohr 53

It All Comes Out In The Wash by N. B. Turner 69

The Selfie Killer by N E Riggs 79

Dick Pic by Don Stoll..89

Photos by Michael Mullen

Hoosier NOIR

Dunn & Dunn

By J. Travis Grundon

Dakota plunged into the dark forest, making his way through the trees, but he tripped, crashing into the earth, and skid forward into a fallen tree. Sticks gouged his face and arms, his head was pounding. He broke free from the branches, untangled himself, and kept running.

How could he be so stupid? There was no way they would let him live after what he had seen.

The strong smell of and honeysuckle filled the air. His only chance was to run through the woods towards the highway, then flag down a passing car. If he could get to the highway, he'd stay in the woods next to the road, keep moving and wait for a car to approach, and get a ride back to town.

When he heard the sound of the truck on the gravel road he knew it wasn't anyone willing to help. He knew that the Dunn boys were hunting him. He dropped and cowered down, pressing his body into the ground. The rich smell of Earth filled his nose. He waited and felt his heartbeat drumming in his ears. He listened until it slowed, as the truck drove further down the road.

Kota was still pressed close to the ground. The trash bag had been lost hours ago and the deadly game of cat and mouse continued into an unknown hour. The Dunn boys knew the area better than him and they were looking for him.

He prayed to God. "Please," he prayed. "Let me live through this."

The truck slowed to a stop again. This time Kota heard doors open and slam shut. They were pretty far away from him, but not far enough. Through the leaves, he could still see the lights of the truck.

It was hard to hear anything of over the growing breeze working through the wooded area. Branches clattered together, dropping sticks to the ground. Leaves rustled and old trees creaked all around him. He breathed with the wind but stayed pressed against the forest floor. He would stay and hide until the truck drove away, or he saw either of the Dunn cousins hiking through the woods to find him.

Dakota Fischer had been harvesting plants from his weed crop near the river but after collecting the two plants into a garbage bag, He saw flashlight beams filtering through the trees. He was sure it was the cops swooping in to bust him for a few marijuana plants. He was frozen with fear until the flashlights moved past him to a spot further down the river. He could see from the moonlight's reflection on the river that Rodney and Wayne Dunn and were dragging something to the river.

It was his trash bag that gave him away. He could eventually see that the Dunn and Dunn had been dragging was a woman. As Rodney took her arms and Wayne took the legs, Kota knew that she was dead. He staggered backward cupping his hands over his mouth, causing the plastic bag to rattle noisily. One of the flashlights turned in his direction and he took off running as fast as his legs would carry him. Wayne and Rodney were cousins and they had a reputation "dealing with" people who pissed them off. Kota wasn't sure if they had seen his face but he didn't want to wait around for them to find him.

He broke out of the trees into a cornfield. There was one field after another after another. Kota navigated through the corn stalks, with leaves slashing at his face, and ready to harvest ears of corn clubbing his body. The rustling of the stalks made it impossible to know what direction he was running or if he was being followed.

He listened hard before running out of the field and into Wayne Dunn's Ford F150. The roll bar, KC lights, and lift kit made it look like a giant Hot Wheels car. It was easily recognizable by the head level collection of TRUMP and NRA bumper stickers and an old, dirty Confederate flag mounted in the bed.

Kota struggled to catch his breath as Rodney Dunn stepped out of the field directly in front of him. He hadn't heard him moving through the corn over the sounds of the trash bag in his hands. The knife in Rodney's hand caught the moonlight. That was when Wayne appeared from the other side brandishing a pump-action shotgun.

Dunn and Dunn dumped two bodies in the river that night.

J. Travis Grundon has served as co-editor and

contributing author of Forrest J Ackerman's Anthology of the Living Dead and Hoosier Noir. He is also the author of two short story collections and one novel. His other work includes two years as an editor and columnist for Rudo Can't Fail: Lucha Libre & Lucha Culture Worldwide. He also writes for Life Along the Wabash.

Interrogating Rex Weiner

Illustration by Ken Avidor

Rex Weiner has been an author, screenwriter, journalist, editor and publisher, first in New York, then in Los Angeles. His work has taken him all over the world. As a journalist, Weiner knew and admired rock critic Lester Bangs, and Rex's taste in noir fiction includes crime novelist Mickey Spillane's classic hardboiled stories. The influences of Spillane, Bangs, comics, AM radio and his own personal experiences on the streets of 1960s-70s New York and 1980s punk rock Hollywood led to the creation of his "rock n' roll detective" named Ford Fairlane.

Most people are familiar with Ford from the 20th Century Fox film, The Adventures of Ford Fairlane, directed by Renny Harlin and released in 1990. This movie featured Andrew Dice Clay in the title role. While the movie became a cult classic, Dice's depiction of Ford was much different from the rock n' roll detective stories originally serialized in the New York Rocker and LA Weekly. For the first time in nearly 40 years, Weiner's original Ford Fairlane stories were published by Rare Bird Books in 2018, titled The (Original) Adventures of Ford Fairlane: The Long Lost Rock n' Roll Detective Stories.

Though Rex Weiner's Hoosier-dom extends mainly to having family in Indianapolis (brother Ken Avidor, the city's well-known illustrator and roving sketch artist), we wanted to talk to him about his latest detective series, Skull Snyder, Mickey Spillane and much more. Fans who only know Weiner from The Adventures of Ford Fairlane have only scratched the surface of his work.

HOOSIER NOIR: Thank you for taking the time to answer a few questions. It seems only logical to start with Ford Fairlane. Is there a chance that we could see a film or TV series based on The (Original) Adventures of Ford Fairlane?

REX WEINER: Anything's possible! The screen rights to the Ford Fairlane character are owned by 20th Century Fox, which was recently purchased by Disney, so unless a brave executive in the Mouse House wants to make a movie about a down n' dirty, streetwise rock n' roll detective, we'll have to wait until they sell the rights to somebody who does. And there are a few producers sniffing around. I doubt the Diceman would be involved, though. He's having too good a time in Vegas.

HN: When might fans get a glimpse of what Ford and his new assistants are up to?

RW: I own the publishing rights, so I'm currently at work on a new Ford Fairlane adventure. He'll be older and, hopefully, wiser—but each time out's a new lesson, of course. He's a cranky geezer—like, maybe, picture Sean Penn, okay? And he's living in a constantly changing, diverse LA that he barely recognizes anymore, He's got two assistants—one is a part-time rapper slash DJ from South Central who swears he's Snoop Dogg's second cousin twice-removed. The other is a young USC grad from Koreatown who is a top female martial arts champ and knows everything about the K-Pop underground scene. When Ford takes on a new client who leads him in over his head, his two assistants step in to help break the case. Anyway, that's how I think the story goes, but I'm in the middle of writing it, so you never know how it's going to turn out. Should have a manuscript by May 2020 and—hopefully—a smart publisher who will release it before the end of the year.

HN: Readers who've checked out your stories in EconoClash Review and Pulp Modern have discovered Skull Snyder. Where did the influence for Snyder come from?

RW: A few years ago, a retired LA County Sheriff's Deputy Homicide cop handed me a stack of old case files he'd worked on—raw reports. Crime scene Polaroids, hand-written interviews, the nitty gritty of murder investigations. "They'll kick my ass if I turn these back in now, so do what you want with them," he said. "Just don't use my name." So my series of stories, loosely based on those files, about a heavily tattooed homicide detective in 1970s LA named Skull Snyder, have begin finding their way into print. The first one, "Death Episode," appeared in EconoClash Review #4 in 2018. The second, "A Hooker, A Pinto, A Gun" appeared in Pulp Modern Vol 2, Issue 4, the same year. I want to thank the editors of those fine publications for taking a chance. Also Jim Thomsen, one of the best editors in the business, who gave the stories a look-over.

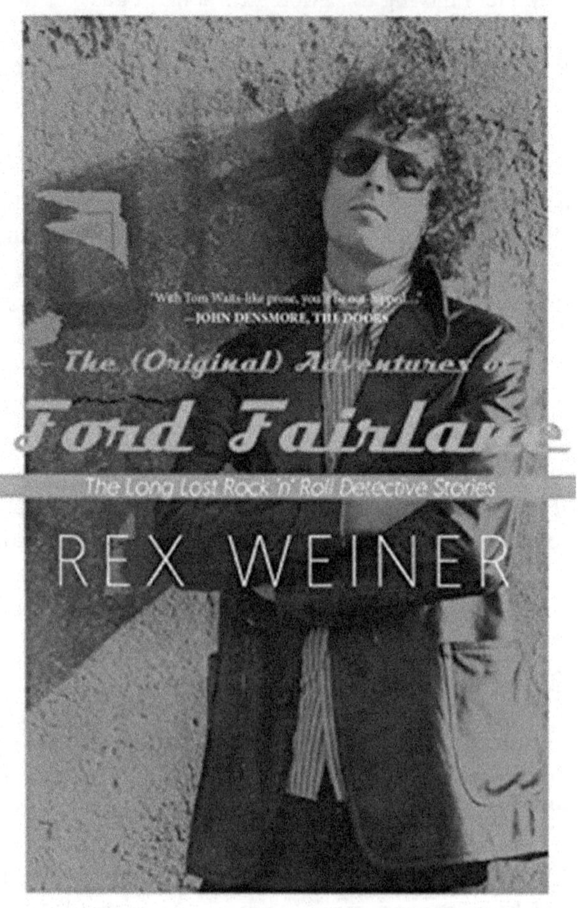

HN: Do you have plans to release a collected "adventures" of Skull Snyder, like your recently published original Ford Fairlane stories?

RW: Eventually, yes. The third Skull Snyder story, "Louella Never Smiled" is actually the first in the series, a kind of "origin story." Again, it's a fictional version of an actual case. It's ready for submission and I'm figuring out where to go with it. A fourth Skull Snyder story is also in the works, with a fifth story ready to assemble. All together, the collected stories will be a portrait of a complicated cop during a complicated era, as well as an experiment in putting flesh on the skeletal remains of a long-forgotten homicide investigation.

HN: Are there any plans for Skull and Ford to cross paths?

RW: Watch out, man. In my universe, that's unavoidable.

HN: How did you get involved with Switchblade?

RW: I had written a story that was too weird to submit anywhere. "On The Way Home" was sort of Twilight Zone, but with a sick edge. So it just sat in my files for about four or five years. I came across Switchblade and quickly concluded that whoever put it together had my kind of crazy. My submission received the quickest acceptance ever, and I'm still thrilled to be in Switchblade Sixx, along with the coolest writers like Travis Richardson, E.F. Sweetman, and I thank Switchblade founder/editor Scotch Rutherford, who has built a noir writers community that he calls the LA Chapter. The man has style and taste.

HN: How would you describe your experiences with the Noir at the Bar events?

RW: Noir at the Bar is a great sort of grass-roots event, if grass could be called "noir." You get to read your work aloud to a group of people who are fans if the genre, not to mention slightly inebriated. Your city sucks if you don't have one of these things. I was honored to be included recently in Albuquerque's first Noir at the Bar this past summer, put together with a great lineup of writers by writer Justin Bendell. In LA, it's the prolific novelist Eric Beetner who organizes it, and it's where I was privileged to launch the Ford Fairlane book. I recommend the experience to writers and readers alike. And have one on me.

HN: Are there any certain writers that you've shared pages with in Switchblade, Pulp Modern, EconoClash Review, or Broadswords and Blasters, that you think everyone needs to know about?

RW: I'm excited about all the writers in these publications, including the one you feature in Hoosier Noir—I'd hate to leave any out—because these publications, and others in the genre, are bringing a whole new crop of writers to a whole new generation of readers, thanks to online and print-on-demand technology. And let's not forget the brave editors/publishers making it all happen.

HN: You've credited Mickey Spillane as an influence on your style. If the opportunity ever presented itself, would you be interested in writing a Mike Hammer story?

RW: Well, I think Skull Snyder and Ford Fairlane have me pretty well tied up, so to speak, and I would fear their jealousy if I took on another PI. And I'm not sure I could do Hammer justice. But I do think Spillane is under-appreciated and with certain outdated attitudes held aside, mainly involving women, he deserves a new appraisal. His stripped-down language is what I admire, and shoot me if you think I'm too high-falutin' literary, but comparisons with Samuel Beckett are not a far stretch, in my opinion.

HN: Have other mystery/ crime fiction authors have had an influence on your work?

RW: The usual—Hammett, Chandler, MacDonald, along with John Le Carré, Patricia Highsmith, Graham Greene, and yes, Ian Fleming with his Bond series, because I grew up during the Cold War, but also those who came long before: Poe, Conrad, Hawthorne, Ambrose Bierce, Conan Doyle, and H.P. Lovecraft whose weirdness infected me as a teenager. Can't bear to read him now, though. Same with Kerouac, Burroughs. and the Beats—they were all following some great mystery, but the results are in and we've moved on, sad to say.

HN: What was the last amazing book you read?

RW: Astounding, by Alec Nevala-Lee, which celebrates the golden age of the sci-fi pulp genre, in which writers like Heinlein, Azimov and Arthur C. Clarke mix it up with whackos like L. Ron Hubbard in the paranoid 1950s, turning out great fiction for pennies, not unlike the present. I make a cameo appearance in the last part where it talks about how I stowed away on a cruise ship to watch the last Apollo moon launch. Got to read it to believe it.

HN: What are some of your thoughts on social media's impact on writers, publishing and marketing a book?

RW: I think social media is great—we get to stay in touch and boost our #writingcommunity, but it can be deadly if it takes time away from #amreading, or worse, #amwriting. There's a whole wide crazy world waiting for you if you just look up from that damn thing in your hand!

Switchblade issue Sixx, Vol. One (2018) featuring On the Way Home by Rex Weiner

This issue also features E.F. Sweetman, Rusty Barnes, and many more!

EconoClash Review No. 4 (2019)
featuring Death Episode by Rex Wiener

econoclash.com

Pulp Modern Vol.2 No. 4 (2019)
featuring A Pinto, a Hooker, a Gun by Rex Weiner

pulp-modern.blogspot.com

UNITED ARTISTS
SWITCHBLADE ISSUE ELEVEN
ALEC CIZAK J.D.GRAVES J.WILSKY
& MORE OCT 4

Author Spotlight: Alec Cizak

Alec Cizak is a writer and filmmaker from Indiana. His books *Down on the Street* and *Breaking Glass* are available from ABC Group Documentation. His short story collection of weird fiction titled *Lake County Incidents*. He is also the editor of the fiction journal *Pulp Modern*.

BREAKING GLASS

ALEC CIZAK

Last Exit Before Toll

By Alec Cizak

"Things can't get worse." Emily said this to Jessica as she lifted her away from a rust-colored dumpster she'd decorated with vomit. "Your body's rejected the poison from the alcohol. Should be a cinch from here."

Jessica shook her head. "No." She tumbled into a brick wall. "I got to get home. I'm totally sorry."

Emily rocked on her feet like a child in need of a potty break. "But Kristoff, he's all into me tonight. Bumped into me twice at the pool tables."

"I'll find my way home." The alley tilted. Jessica remembered a funhouse she'd negotiated as a child at the Lake County Fair. Her brain turned somersaults and she collapsed. Emily jammed her hands under her armpits and hoisted her to her feet. She held her up as they wobbled toward the street. She leaned her against a No Parking sign and asked to use her phone. Jessica said, "Ran out of juice when I was on the toilet, playing the bubble game."

"I see." Emily rummaged through her purse.

Headlights paled the women and a yellow cab pulled to the curb. The passenger window buzzed down and the driver leaned over the seat. "Hey ladies," he said. "Need a ride?"

Jessica grabbed the No Parking sign and reached for the back door. Emily stopped her. "Dude's, like, *way* past old. Gray hair. Black clothes. Only serial killers dress like that." She ducked to speak with the cabbie. "We're waiting for an Uber."

The cabbie laughed. "I'm right here. Cheaper and safer." He pointed to a laminated card posted on the glovebox with his name and photo. Looked like a mug shot.

"We'll stick with progress, if you don't mind." Emily slapped the roof of the cab and told the driver to move along. He peered over his wire-framed grandpa glasses, reminded Jessica of her father, any time she said something he deemed stupid. Finally, Emily said, "We need to get the cops?"

Shaking his head, the cabbie chuckled once more. He turned the taxi around and parked at O'Neal's, a pub across the street.

Emily found her phone and called for an Uber. She argued about the fare. The door to the bar opened and Kristoff Ronin, a DJ she'd been trying to bag for a couple of weeks, poked his head out. "You girls okay? Brummer and I were thinking of heading to the gardens at Valpo to smoke a bowl and look at the sky. Listen to some tunes, yo."

"Sounds awesome." Emily positioned Jessica against the No Parking sign again. "You going to be cool?" She slipped her a twenty-dollar bill. "That doesn't cover it, tell the driver to go fuck himself. 'Peak hours.' Give me a break. Capitalist scumbags." She gave her a kiss on the cheek and started for the bar. "I don't want to miss this." Then she stepped inside and left Jessica in the cold.

The sidewalk rocked like a boat on Lake Shafer as Jessica's head rolled back and forth. A compact car, looked like a purple Prius, rolled up. The driver yelled from his side, "Hey there!"

Jessica tumbled into the street, caught herself on the trunk, and inched her way to the driver's window. "You the Uber guy?" She hoped she hadn't slurred too much. She'd heard stories about grabby jerks molesting lit passengers. This one didn't look too awful, though—young, lumberjack beard, and long hair tied in a bun on the top of his head.

He said, "Name's Truco." He unlocked the back door and nodded over his shoulder.

Jessica got in. The vehicle smelled like mildew on cardboard. She gave him her address. "Just outside Lublin," she said. "It's easy to find." As the car merged into traffic, she noticed a baseball bat on the passenger seat. Seemed like it'd been smeared with blood. "You want your money now?"

The driver took a deep breath and said, "No rush." He turned on the radio. "Kind of music you into?"

"Whatever's good," she said.

Dubstep pounded the speakers. The driver shouted something Jessica couldn't understand, then made eye contact with her in the rearview and smiled. Frankly, young guys with lumberjack beards had never bothered her. If they mustered the courage to approach her, they always looked down, as though embarrassed by their libidos.

The car picked up speed as the driver took the I-65 ramp toward Chicago. Not the way she would have chosen, but, oh well. The doors rattled as the music intensified. The exit for Lublin passed. Jessica tapped the driver on his shoulder. "You should have gotten off there!"

He turned around, bobbed his head with the dubstep, the grin on his face growing as the car raced away from Lake County, toward Gary and Chicago beyond. Jessica looked for the driver's identification card. The dumbass didn't have a GPS or anything. He hadn't even pasted one of those Uber stickers to his window.

The driver took an exit just across the Illinois border, the last one before the first toll booth. Streetlights disappeared. Beech trees blotted out the sky. Darkness filled the Prius. Jessica cursed the possibility of having to walk home from there. She'd post a scathing review of the driver on the Internet the *moment* she plugged in her phone.

MACABRE STORIES BY **ALEC CIZAK**

LAKE COUNTY INCIDENTS

Destroyers

By Alec Cizak

You heard about Brian Klein, right? No? Sweet Jesus, boy learned himself a lesson. I know, I know, how's it possible he learned anything, freeloading in his mama's basement? Just mooching off her like a parasite. No accountability for nothing. No job. Well, shoot, what you expect? Brian's got a bachelor's *and* a master's in English. How you going to study the language everyone already speaks by nature and expect to have any skills worth a damn? Yes, yes, he *could* dump coffee in a mug, like Shirley Baker's girl LaDonna does, over there at the café on Seventh Street. But Haggard ain't Chicago, and, well, we just don't need that many English majors to serve drinks in the morning.

But don't let me get sidewise on this here story. Not this soon. So, Brian Klein's livelihood, if you could call it such, involved tracking down culprits on the *Twitter* and *Facebook* that don't sit right with the finger-wagging crowd. Brian likes to look into folks who've been exalted for various deeds and find out if they got any dirt lingering under their toenails. For instance, Brian was one of the first to blab about Mayor Koski's flirtation with marijuana back in the 1980s, when the mayor was a student up there at fancy Northwestern. Wouldn't have bothered folks none too much had Koski not gone on the tube a week earlier and claimed Hoosiers were too stupid to handle legalized weed. Much of a point as he might have had, that picture Brian uncovered, the one of an eighteen-year old Steve Koski smoking a joint at a Dead show in Cleveland, well, it rendered the mayor a hypocrite. This society we've fashioned since the Internet became king, shoot, we just love to ridicule anyone for any possible wrongdoing. Don't much matter that Steve Koski's looking down the barrel of fifty and, having several decades between now and his college days, may have changed his mind once or twice on moral issues. Brian found some dirt on him, slung it like a cow paddy, and called it a major revelation. I suppose you might christen this the Age of the Lazy Inquisition. I doubt Brian Klein climbed out of his pajamas before making his way across his mama's basement floor, traveling from his bed to his computer, before doing a search or two on Google and finding that picture of our idiot mayor.

But here I go again, started in one direction and veering off in another. Bear with me, my friends. We got time, might as well use it. So, Brian, as always, is spending his day surfing the Internet, checking up on all the hot news stories, you know, things people talk about for three minutes before the next headline comes along. He sees this bit about an ancient football hero from Lublin named Cory Bunker. That's right, old Bonks. Surely you all remember how he took Lublin to State back in '90. Lost to them rich boys from Carmel. Well, Bonks used to have serious control issues, no different than a lot of young men playing linebacker for an Indiana high school, knowing full well they aren't good enough for a scholarship, even to a crappy MAC school like Ball State, and sure not good enough to ever play in the pros. They get used to the crowds on Friday nights, egging them on to flatten running backs and cripple wide receivers. Then the glory's over. Pretty girls don't throw themselves at them no more. Carl Fork stops giving them discounts at Lake County Automotive. These boys wind up pumping gas or selling used cars. If they're lucky, they get a construction gig that twists their spines and puts a fair amount of cash in their pockets. Bonks, he took a job sweeping up the stadium at Valpo, cutting the grass, getting it ready for games on Saturday. In the wintertime, he mopped floors in the lecture halls and scrubbed the bleachers and the hardwood in the basketball arena. Married that chunky Joyner girl from Pawpaw Grove. She squeezed out a couple of sons who got into the pain pills when they were teens and died before they hit twenty. Mind you, when we get to the part where Brian Klein stuck his nose in Bonks' business, note how Brian didn't pay no mind to these particular ills in Bonks' tragic biography.

Well, Bonks was driving home one evening. He sees some youngster, a sixth-grader named Peyton Sipes, getting pushed around by a flock of older boys. They'd knocked Peyton off his Schwinn, if that's what the kids are riding these days, and they'd ripped his backpack off his shoulders and tossed his schoolbooks all around him like a mini Stonehenge. They were closing in like hyenas, getting ready to damage him physical-wise. Bonks pulls over. Gets out of his '96 Chevelle, the brown one with a floor so rusted his wife's got to keep her legs up or she'll be shuffling her feet like she's on the old *Flintstones* cartoon show. He shoves that squeaky, stubborn car door out of his way and rushes over to Peyton and the bullies. It don't take him three seconds to scatter those older boys in every direction. Just showed them that fist of his that used to punish the best tailbacks in the state and growled a line or two about bashing in their skulls.

Now, it so happens a little girl named Tina Bunting had her cellphone out and decided to film the whole thing for prosperity's sake. She puts her little documentary on *Facebook* and, wouldn't you know it, millions of people pass it around. Goes viral, as fellows who look like lumberjacks but work in bookstores like to say. Next thing Bonks knows; he's being interviewed by all them big news outlets. Fancy reporters put microphones in front of his face and ask him how it feels to be a hero. Well, Bonks, being a humble type from Lake County, he blushes and insists it weren't nothing any ordinary, decent human being wouldn't have done. But it don't stop there. Greg Bickle, yes, yes, Greg Bickle, the quarterback for the Chicago Bears, he gives old Bonks a call and asks if he wants to sit in a corporate box in Soldier Field the next time them filthy Packers roll through. Victor Pacheco, yes, *the* Victor Pacheco, the guy who plays Astroman in them comic book movies, he sends Bonks a personal Twit, or Tweet, or whatever the hell it's called, letting him know how all them rich folks in Hollywood thinks Bonks is just as peachy as grape-flavored cocaine. Point being, that little gesture by Bonks, taking time out of his miserable life to make sure Peyton Sipes didn't get his ribs kicked in by a stink of cowards, that smidgeon of kindness made Bonks a celebrity for the customary five minutes the Internet grants us lowly working folk who don't live in L.A. or New York. If you read the various reports, the initial reports, that is, of what Bonks had to say throughout all this, you'll see it never inflated his head. I guess playing high school football in Indiana taught him all the consequences of taking the flattery of a mob too serious. And his time in the spotlight would have ended just like that, on a nice, positive note, were it not for Betty Klein's mooching, adult son, whose college degrees made him so damn incompetent he can't even secure a job putting potato chips on the shelf at the local Walmart.

You see, Brian Klein hates himself. That's the only diagnosis I can conjure to explain why he does what he does. Why he did what he did. And when a man hates himself, well, he can't stand to see another man's life made decent, even if it's just for a flash, a moment of time so insignificant it would have been forgotten the very next week. Folks like Brian Klein, they sense beauty in this world, and their first inclination is to destroy it.

Brian Klein got to work hounding dirt on Bonks. He dialed up his account at Transparency dot com, that site that finds every bit of info ever documented about another human being. Real nosy enterprise, you ask me. Didn't take Brian long to stumble across that incident between Bonks and Mel Spivey. If you don't recall it right off the top of your head, don't beat yourself up. Most folks let it drift and drown in the past since Bonks did his time and demonstrated, public-wise, his remorse for setting Mel Spivey's nose a hair to the left. You remember now, don't you? The Old Oaken Bucket, 1990. Bonks grew up in a house worshipping the Boilermakers. Didn't much matter that neither Bonk's dad nor his granddad had attended college, let alone Purdue. They'd developed a cult-like attachment to the football team and, as such, were obliged to loathe and despise the, generally, woeful Indiana Hoosiers. Except, of course, the Hoosiers came up to Lafayette that year and whooped the Boilers by two touchdowns. In the parking lot, after the game, Bonks bumped into Mel Spivey, who'd worn his crimson and white gear and couldn't help but say something to him. What kind of lousy squad loses to the Hoosiers? he'd said, grinning that goofy, toothless grin he'd earned mouthing off to Drew Richards at prom, senior year. Why the hell anyone from Lake County would root for IU is beyond me, but, you know, Mel always did his own thing. Guess that's how he ended up running the mortuary on Fourth Street. Well, Bonks, he didn't take to getting razzed right after seeing the Boilermakers lose. He brings that brick-sized fist of his back and lands it at a perfect angle, collapsing Mel Spivey's nose to the side, like folding a page in a book. Blood spills all over, so much a hot dog vendor nearby used an entire package of napkins helping Mel get it under control. They wheeled Mel Spivey to the emergency room at St. Francis and, later that night, Mel gave a statement to the police and agreed to press charges. Bonks pleaded guilty and served a two-month sentence plus probation. He paid his debt in the form of community service, changing diapers at the Rosehill retirement community. Like I said, folks would have forgotten the whole thing, except maybe Mel Spivey, who's reminded of it every time he looks at his gangly, bony face in the mirror. It just so happens Mel's cousin Bernice worked for the *Journal & Courier*, and he convinced her to write a teeny-tiny little story about it, way back in 1990, that appeared on the last page of a Tuesday edition, next to the obituaries.

Brian Klein found that article. He found the police report, the arrest record, and the court documents. He couldn't log on to *Twitter* fast enough to post what he considered the *truth* about Cory "Bonks" Bunker. He twittered, or tweeted, or whatever the hell you folks call it, that Bonks was, in fact, a bully himself. The big corporate-controlled news outlets, ever eager to match the self-righteous indignation trickling down the average *Twitter* feed, picked up the story. Outlets that hadn't even reported the first part, the part about Bonks being a hero, ran with Brian Klein's correction, painting Bonks as the meanest sonofabitch who ever came up in Lake County, or Indiana, or the Midwest, or America itself. The twittiots of the land allowed Brian Klein to alter their previous impression of Bonks, to turn admiration into hatred. Them celebrities, soft enough in the brain to let an invisible mob influence them, rescinded their nice offers. All over a parking lot ruckus from thirty years ago.

Unfortunately for Brian Klein, the torch and pitchfork chorus on *Twitter* had enough influence to convince the useless bureaucrats at Valpo to fire Bonks. The very last thing that man needed in this economy, in this brutal, stupid, disgusting world we've created. His wife don't work no more on account of her foot getting run over by a forklift at Liberty Steel. The hell they going to do now? Bonks figured, best thing for him would be free room and board.

Well now, after all that, we can get to the crux of the story, the meat of the matter, if you will. Brian Klein, he heard a knock at his mother's front door just about a week ago. No doubt he'd been basking in the glory of bringing down another, in his mind, corrupt human being, someone whose life had carried just a little more weight than his. He had to compose himself, put on some decent clothes over his pajamas, and make that rough trek up them creaky, wooden steps in his mama's basement. He opens the door and, wouldn't you know it, there's Cory Bunker, Bonks, one-time hero, permanent goat, just smirking. He couldn't have asked for a more convenient solution. He said, You Brian Klein? Now, I'd just about pay anything to be able to get in a time machine and have a front row seat, watching Brian Klein soil his pajamas. He stuttered and stammered, apparently tried to lie, say he was someone else. So Bonks tells him, I seen your picture on your *Facebook* page. I know who you are.

Brian started cussing Bonks in that gibberish you only hear on college campuses, calling him a reactionary, telling him all about his privilege, calling him an oppressor, if you can believe it.

Bonks, he just grabs Brian Klein by that scraggly, disgusting lumberjack beard of his, yanks him closer, winds up, and lands that monster fist on the side of Brian Klein's face. Neighbors claimed they could hear Brian's jaw crack from inside their homes. Bonks rearranged his *entire* skull. Dented his face like that painting of that guy screaming on a bridge. Then he turned right around and went to Haggard PD to confess. Word I've heard is he plans on representing himself in court, thinks it's the best way to get himself a nice, cozy cell down in Pendleton.

As for Brian Klein, neighbors said he ain't made one move toward finding himself a job so he can detach from his mother's generous nipple. They did, however, rejoice the morning they watched him wheel his computer desk, complete with the computer on top of it, out to the trash bin in the alley behind his mother's house. Maybe, just maybe, without the Internet giving Brian Klein crumbs of glory, he might start thinking the way humans is *supposed* to think. He might start looking for beauty in the world and, perhaps, upon finding it, he just may choose to leave it be.

FirstCityBooks.com/HoosierNoir

@HoosierNoir

Descent

By Preston Lang

The chief of police seemed to treat everything I had to say with just a little bit of contempt.

"How long has he been gone, Mr. Kent?" he asked me.

"Hal never came home last night."

"You guys had a fight. Am I right?"

"No. Nothing like that."

Chief Lohta tore open a packet of sugar. It was a lot of work for him to dump it into his coffee. Men like him made me nervous—thick Midwesterners, over fifty, with authority but not too much money. They always seemed to blame me for everything they didn't have.

"Did you try calling him?" he asked.

"He left his phone behind."

"When did he leave?"

"After 9:30, almost 10 maybe. He went out. To the store."

"What did he need from the store so late?"

"Just some things. Yogurt."

"Yogurt?"

He gave the word a little goose. Like only gays eat yogurt? What the hell? This is the 21st century. Everybody eats yogurt.

"I was supposed to get it earlier, but I forgot, so—"

"So you *did* have a fight?"

"No. It wasn't a—fight. Not exactly."

"Sure, it was. He was upset he had to go out to the store in the middle of the night, now he's teaching you a lesson."

"So what am I supposed to do?"

"Wait. Either he comes back to you or he doesn't."

"What if he had an accident? Maybe he needs help."

"If anything turns up—hospitals, morgues—we'll let you know. But this kind of thing happens. A roommate takes off after some kind of yogurt fight. That's not something we handle."

"He's not my roommate. He's my husband."

"Did he pack a bag when he left?"

"No. I mean—most of his stuff, he left behind."

"Most of it?"

"He took his jacket. Maybe some other stuff is missing. But really most of—"

"Okay, he took his jacket? It was over 80 degrees last night, right? And he was just popping out to get some yogurt. Why would he bring a jacket?"

"I don't—I don't believe he would leave me."

"Look, either he'll come back to you, or he won't."

"You must be really proud of that line because that's the second time you've used it."

"I don't need the sarcasm, Mr. Kent."

"Well, you need something to motivate you to do your job."

Was it a good idea to antagonize the chief of police? I'd thought a lot about that before going in. I needed him to dislike me and see me as an annoyance, but I didn't want to make a full-blown enemy. I felt like I'd walked the line just right. But what did I know? Maybe he'd seen right through me the moment I walked in the door.

* * *

The night before, I'd forgotten to buy yogurt—5.3-ounce Dannon blueberry. Hal needed two of them every morning or his whole day would be thrown off. His whole day of surfing the net, thinking of reasons why he couldn't paint, maybe calling up Allison to play tennis at her club. For all this he needed his yogurt.

It was unusually hot for May, and the AC in the car wasn't working, so we were both a little annoyed already. He asked me if I'd bought the yogurt—knowing full well I'd forgotten. The Schnuck's was closed, so I ducked into one of those gas station delis, but they didn't have blueberry. He looked at me like this was some enormous victory for him. There was still the 24-hour Superette on the other side of town, but he struck viciously while he had the advantage. My incompetence. My age. My failures. I took a turn on the road that ran back out to the state park.

"Where are you going?"

I didn't say a word for three miles.

"Turn the car around, you fat, old hag."

I parked on the side of the road.

"Shut the hell up. Now," I said.

"Oh, look at this tough guy."

"Don't push me. Not tonight."

So, of course, he pushed as hard as he could. Out came all my faults and inadequacies, and then a teenage humiliation that I didn't even remember telling him about. Before I knew it, my hands were around his throat, and I was squeezing. Right through the hissing. Right through the scratching at my arms and my ribcage. Until he stopped moving altogether. Then I was alone with the body of this man I'd once loved more than anything in the world. The man I'd married in a bad Unitarian ceremony that cost more than I wanted to pay. Now he was nothing—cargo, meat, an express lane prop.

My first thought was to drive down to Kentucky, to his Mom's house. Dump the body on her porch, drive home, get good and drunk, then wait for a healthy slice of *Que Sera Sera*. But looking out over the side of the road, I saw a lush canopy of bushes, and I thought how cool it would be to watch an Acura drop a hundred feet in the moonlight. I'd always hated this car—his car—and thought it was more than he needed for the little he had to do.

At first, I wasn't really thinking of it as a way to conceal a crime, but something must have kicked in because I took his cell phone out of his pocket but left the money and his wallet. Then I pushed the car off the road, over the shoulder toward the edge. The car moved steadily for about ten feet then all of a sudden it stalled. I didn't even check to see if it was snagged on something. I just backed up and charged like a linebacker. It went off the cliff, and for a second I thought I was going down with it. But I didn't.

It wasn't a busy road at night. Nothing had passed in either direction since I'd stopped. Down, over the edge, I couldn't see the car. I could see the brush clearly by the light of a nearly full moon, but the car seemed to have plunged under the thick green of late spring. I walked home, off to the shoulder of the road, ducking behind the low corn both times I heard a car approach.

In the shower, I saw deep scratches on my forearms and side, but a long-sleeved tee shirt covered all that. I took the Toyota—my car—out to the Superette.

The woman behind the counter was a familiar, friendly face.

"Did you see Hal? You know—red-haired guy, comes in here a lot. My husband."

"Tonight, you mean?"

"Yeah. He came out to buy some yogurt."

"Dannon blueberry?" She smiled.

"Yeah. Was he here tonight?"

"No. I didn't see him. And I've been here since 4."

I went over to the dairy section. They had blueberry. I bought four containers.

The next morning, I called in sick to work and then drove to the state park. On the way back I stopped briefly and looked over the side where I'd shoved the car. I could see only a tiny sliver of the underside. If you didn't know it was down there, you probably wouldn't notice it. And it would only get better hidden over the summer.

When I got home, I called Allison—the woman Hal played tennis with occasionally, probably his only friend in town. She was groggy and confused. I explained that I hadn't seen Hal since the night before. Had she heard anything?

"What? No, I haven't. Is everything all right?"

"I'm sure it's nothing, but—just let me know if you hear from him."

Then I put on a suit, went in to see Chief Lohta, and did a pretty good impression of the kind of man whose husband will run off on him after a petty argument. It wasn't until late that night that I called Hal's mother and asked if she'd heard from her son.

"He left you? Good."

"I don't know where he is."

"Probably left you. I'll tell you something else: if I do hear from him, I certainly won't call you up."

"Mrs. Ellis, I'm trying to—"

"You're the one who wrecked him. Got him twisted up in that *marriage* of yours? Kind of a sick joke, isn't it?"

"I just want to see him again."

Then I started crying. For real. Honest emotion can rise out of the baldest lies.

"You think I want to listen to that? Boo Hoo Hoo." she laughed. "Everything you got, you had coming to you. Don't you call me ever again."

She hung up and I cried for another two minutes, then stopped. I'd done everything I could and kept all the pieces straight. It was time to live my life and hope for the best. I didn't have any friends at work, so I doubted anyone would notice a difference in me. They handed me the same impossible files they always did, and I spent my days searching through them, looking for inconsistencies—columns that didn't match. It was soothing work that kept me busy. Night was the only real problem. I slept in the living room now, facing the wall. There were too many things I didn't want to have to look at.

A week after the disappearance, I called the chief again and asked for an update. He was civil but terse. Nothing had come in. I called the next week, then two weeks later. Nothing. Nothing, at all. The car lay in the bush. I drove past it once in July, and it was completely covered in green. No one had stumbled across it. I began to look for jobs out on the west coast. Maybe live in a real city—Portland, San Francisco, LA. Maybe live a real life.

Allison called every day and came over most evenings. At first I resented her, but after a while she became a kind of comfort. She brought me Tupperware full of excellent lasagna and even got me to play a little tennis. When I knew her only as Hal's friend, I'd assumed she was an airhead, a silly ditz. But now spending time alone with her, I saw that she had depth and patience.

"I love this house," she said one hot summer night on my front porch.

"You mean he'd be crazy to leave such a beautiful home?"

"No, I don't mean that. But what is he living on?"

"Maybe he wanted to start over from scratch," I said. "He's younger than we are. He can still do that. A basement apartment in New York and minimum wage side gig might be the kind of romantic idea an artist gets into his head."

"It just seems so strange. Maybe you should hire a detective. Hal could be in a hospital somewhere. Maybe he needs our help."

"If that's true, they would have found me by now."

And then one evening at the end of August, without warning Allison brought a psychic down from Indianapolis into my home. A fit, middle-aged woman in a green tracksuit and visor. As much as I wanted to throw her out of my house by her hair, I couldn't quite do it. She was formidable in the way a performer on stage frequently manages to grab a certain amount of unearned power.

"I have to warn you that I will be honest. I provide deep compassion, but I'm also unflinchingly honest. Are you prepared for that?"

"Sure."

"You say—*Sure*. A lot of people say Sure. I don't want to get halfway down the road and then discover that you are not comfortable with truth."

"I'm comfortable with the truth."

"Good. Your husband was a small man, slender."

"He was. Is."

She went on for a while giving me obvious facts about my

Hal. There was something disturbing about all of it, but I couldn't quite find it in myself to laugh at her as she deserved. For just a moment, I wondered if she knew something.

"And there was trouble in your marriage. *He* felt all of this more deeply than you did. To you it may have seemed as if you had occasional quarrels or occasional frostiness. That's not how he saw it. You probably thought you had provided him with this beautiful home, a comfortable life—that he needed nothing else. But he did need something else. And you may not be pleased to hear this, but right now, he's where he has to be. Will he come back to you? That's not something you can *expect* to happen."

"Where is he?"

"Far from here. And while he's not content, and his life isn't perfect, he is working towards his own fulfillment. I suggest that you do the same."

I nodded significantly. The psychic asked for a glass of ice water. Then she left.

"I'm so sorry," Allison said. "I thought it might help."

"It didn't."

I was angry, and I nearly told her to leave, but then she giggled.

"I'm kind of surprised she didn't say that she saw Hal near water."

"Why would she say that?"

"It's what all the psychics say about missing people."

"Why did you even bring her here?"

"I don't know. Are you mad?"

I didn't say anything. For a second, I felt my fist clench— ready to throw a punch. But when she opened a bottle of wine, I let her pour me a glass and tell me random things about my husband. How hopeless he was at tennis. How sweet he was when she broke up with some arrogant lawyer. But then she said Hal was always a little mean and that he really had no talent when it came to painting.

"Well, he never really got around to finishing anything," I said.

"No, he just had no talent." she poured herself another glass. "Hey, have you started eating blueberry yogurt?"

"Why?"

"You've got four of them in the fridge."

"Oh, leftover from . . ."

"Right, but I thought he went to get the yogurt that night because you were all out?"

"Yeah, then I went looking for him. I went to the Superette

and asked if they'd seen him. I bought four containers just because I was there."

"Oh, that makes sense. More sense than—I don't know—you started trying to eat like him."

"That would be very silly."

"How did you know the psychic wasn't telling the truth?"

"I don't believe in psychics."

"Sure, but I watched you while she was talking. You were open to it for a while, but when she started saying he was trying to fulfill himself somewhere, you didn't even consider the possibility that it could be true."

"It could be true, but I don't feel like I had anything to learn from a cheap performer like her."

Allison didn't call the next day—or the day or the week after that. Summer became fall, and I got an offer from a firm in Seattle. Same work, better location, more money. I had to sell the house, which would be a pain, but it started to look like I might have everything wrapped up and behind me by the New Year. Then the Friday after Thanksgiving, a hiker's dog found a human foot. It was chewed up in places and partially decomposed. The hiker thought it was some kind of gag at first. When he reported it to the police, they searched the area and found the overturned car, nearly a mile away. Soon after that they found the rest of Hal, scattered throughout the woods. It wasn't clear whether the body had been thrown on impact or whether animals had climbed into the car and pulled it out. Before Chief Lohta contacted me, there were pictures online—the overturned car, a few of the body parts. I called him with real fury.

"If you had started looking for him—"

"Mr. Kent."

"No, you let me finish. If you'd started looking for him when I first told you he was missing, maybe we could have found him, and maybe we could have saved him."

"Mr. Kent."

"And aren't there supposed to be guard rails, proper lighting?"

"It seems likely that he'd been drinking."

"Why does that seem likely? You have any evidence of that at all?"

"Mr. Kent—"

"His body was just out there? Eaten by animals? Pictures of his intestines are all over the internet before you even had the courtesy—"

"Mr. Kent, I am warning you—"

"No, you're not warning me of anything. I'm done with you. You're worthless."

Two weeks later, Lohta called and asked me to come down to the station. I refused.

"Tell me what you have to say over the phone."

He exhaled impatiently and told me he was coming over. I told him to stay away, that I didn't want to see him again, but when he rang the doorbell, I let him inside.

"I heard you were leaving town," he said.

"I've got a job offer, yes."

"Out in Seattle?"

"What do you have to say to me?"

"Medical examiner seems to think that your husband was strangled to death."

"What?"

"Someone strangled him in the car then pushed him off a cliff."

"Who would do that?"

"You have a guess, Mr. Kent?"

"This is all based on a body that's been out in the open for half a year?"

"Amazing what science does when you let it."

"And you think he'd been drinking?"

"No, who told you that?"

He'd forgotten already. He was a liar. The information from the medical examiner was a lie—or nothing they could prove. This was all a bluff.

"Officer, please get out of my house, now."

"I would think you'd want to help us find your lover's killer. Now, what's got you all aflutter, Mr. Kent?"

"I'm not aflutter. I don't trust you, and I want you to leave my house."

"I got a call from a woman a month back. She said she had information about you. What you might have done to your man."

"That sounds like some real nonsense."

"Yeah, I didn't think too much about it, until today when I heard back from the examiner. Look, maybe he got you angry— the old yogurt spat in the car. You just meant to quiet him down. It got a little out of control. We can probably call that manslaughter. If you hold to your lies, it's murder one. Jury votes on your death. You think they're going to like you? Has anyone ever liked you?"

"Yes. Hal loved me. Then he died in an accident, his

internal organs were eaten by animals, and the chief of police insulted me in my own home.”

* * *

Nothing was made public about Hal being strangled. From what I was able to figure out, it seemed like the sort of thing an examiner could guess at but not prove in court, not after the amount of time and damage to the body that Hal had. I arranged for the cremation of what they could round up. The Unitarians called and asked if I wanted any kind of ceremony, but I turned them down. If Hal’s mom had any thoughts on the matter, she didn’t share them with me. I didn’t hear from Lohta either, so I lived my life like I was leaving town on the 28th of December.

On the 24th Allison called me.

“Sorry,” she said.

“About what?”

“Hal. Being dead.”

“I’m very busy.”

“You’re moving to Seattle, right? Unless you have to stay here for the investigation.”

“There’s no investigation. He went off a cliff.”

“But they think he was strangled first.”

“Who told you that?”

“Everyone’s heard about it. That along with someone telling the chief she heard you saying you’d killed Hal.”

“Well, that person is lying.”

“I went to the Superette a while back and talked to Nancy. She works weeknights. She remembered you came in looking for Hal. And you bought some yogurt like you said. She also said there were scratches on your wrist and on the back of your neck.”

“I doubt that.”

“No one from the police has even thought to talk to her, and she’s not the sort to seek them out. But it wouldn’t be hard to put them together, you know?”

“I don’t see how any of this would amount to anything.”

“Maybe it wouldn’t, but little things can lead to bigger things. Maybe someone else tells them you admitted it all to her one drunken night.”

* * *

The realtor argued with me— *it’s almost like you’re giving away the house.* But I got her to understand that I wanted a deal as quick as possible, cut all ties with my personal tragedy. And Allison could put down forty percent cash that afternoon if need be. I had asked her a few times to come over and discuss the terms,

45

but she always turned me down and said there was nothing we couldn't do by phone. I thought she was silly to fear me. I only wanted to talk, but maybe she was right. The night I killed Hal, I thought we were just going to have an ugly conversation on the side of the road. But if that were true, why did I drive three miles from civilization before parking the car and provoking the worst in him? Why had I stopped at the perfect spot to drop the car? I think there was a hidden part of me always at work on my most serious problem. Allison would get the house, but I wondered what that hidden part would be able to arrange for the future.

Preston Lang's short work has appeared in Thuglit, All Due Respect, and Betty Fedora. He's also published three novels with Down and Out Press and writes a regular column for WebMd.com.

BAD
Decisions

Vincennes Writers Group

Think you've made some bad decisions?
Check these out.

Available from First City Books
FirstCityBooks.com

The Iceman

by Les Edgerton

I shot her.

Twice.

The first time so she'd feel it, get the picture.

I wanted to talk to her a bit before I finished.

I told you, you didn't know me, I said.

You kept giving me that stupid grin and saying—I lived with you for twenty-five years. I know you.

But you don't, I said. See?

Then, I shot her the second time. The first time it was a gutshot and the second I put a hole in her forehead.

I imagine she believed me now, I thought. For a few seconds anyway. Between the first bullet and the second.

She never said anything, either time. But then, she didn't need to. Her face said it all. She realized I was telling the truth after all.

After the second shot, the one that quieted her for good, I sat there awhile, waiting for the emotion to come, but it never did. Not even a general feeling. Nothing. Nada. That was what I was trying to tell her—had always been trying to tell her.

I sat there, in the chair across from her. From what wasn't her any more. Now it was just a body. I thought about what memories I'd carry with me of her after twenty-five years of marriage.

All I could come up with was our nightly routine. At nine sharp, each evening, we'd turn off everything downstairs and come up to bed. I'd go in the bathroom first, and sit on the stool, lid down, and read something, usually a novel. I'd have my last cigarette of the day. Take my pills. Open the window so the smoke would go out. If it was summer, I'd close it before I left to keep the air conditioning in. Same thing in the winter, for the furnace. Those times when neither was on, I'd just leave it up.

I'd leave a cigarette for her on the sink counter. We kept a lighter there, all the time.

I'd go to bed, turn down my side and climb in. She'd usually have the TV on, the remote tossed on my side of the bed. That was because she'd go to sleep before me. I was a night owl. From my days in the joint. I couldn't go to sleep without TV or some kind of noise going on. Since our neighborhood was quiet, it was the TV's job to get me to sleep.

She'd go in the bathroom and smoke the cigarette I'd left for her.

You may wonder why she didn't have her own. Years ago, she'd quit. Only she hadn't. She just quit buying cigarettes. She just smoked mine.

Depending on the day of the week, she'd have whatever she liked that day on. On Thursdays, it was always Cops, either a rerun or a new episode. If Cops wasn't on, it would be Court TV for a long time and then ID. Both featured murder cases.

After she finished her cigarette, she'd come in, turn down her side, throw the covers off and lay there. For what seemed all of our married life, she had heat attacks as soon as she came to bed. Menopause, she said, but it was sure a long menopause. It lasted for at least the last fifteen years of our marriage.

Until I shot her. Twice.

It just irritated me, her saying she knew me.

Now she does.

I went pulled the blanket up over her face. You see, I said to her. I really was the Iceman. You should have believed me. All I ever asked from you was respect.

I went into the bathroom and there was the cigarette I'd left her. I smoked it all the way down.

No sense in letting it go to waste.

Les Edgerton served a little over 2 years in Pendleton in the sixties on a 2-5 burglary charge (plea-bargained down from 82 counts of second-degree burglary, a count of armed robbery, a count of strong-armed robbery, and a count of possession with intent to sell). When he was in the joint, then-President Johnson declared Pendleton to be "the single worst prison in the U.S." Les agrees with that assessment...

Since then, Les has earned a B.A. (With Honors of Distinction) from Indiana University and an MFA in Writing from

Vermont College. He has published 20 books, taught creative writing at various universities, including the UCLA Writer's Program, St. Francis University, and served as Writer-in-Residence at the University of Toledo and at Trine University. His work has been nominated for the Pushcart Prize, O. Henry Award, Edgar Allan Poe Award (short story category), PEN/Faulkner Award, Jesse Jones Book Award, Derringer Award, Violet Crown Book Award (was awarded a Special Citation for his novel *The Death of Tarpons*), and others. A screenplay of his was a semifinalist in the Nichol's Foundation Awards. The *NY Times* review of his story collection, *Monday's Meal*, compared him favorably to Raymond Carver.

The Haunted Crave Knowing

By J. Rohr

Rebecca finished her cigarette. The dark cloud she sighed matched her mood. Bills on the coffee table called to mind a ticking time bomb.

Topping off her vodka rocks, she heard the doorbell. She considered ignoring it — zero desire to deal with more repo men. Though what remained for them to take, she glanced at the few bits of furniture figuring the proverbial pound of flesh.

The doorbell stopped chiming. Knocking sounded. However, not the door rattling pound of debt collectors. Rather the soft tap of someone unsure if they should.

Rebecca answered it. On the front steps stood a young woman in a blue blouse and bell bottom jeans.

"What do you want?" Rebecca said.

The woman flinched, "Uh, I'm sorry. Is Doug Conover here?"

"Why?"

She said, "I was told he could help me."

"He can't help anybody anymore. He's dead."

The woman's face fell, "Sorry to bother you."

Rebecca watched her walk away. Part of her wanted to let the woman leave.

"What sort of trouble are you in?" Rebecca asked.

The woman stopped. She chewed her lip. Rebecca sipped her vodka.

The woman said, "My name's Joyce. My brother was murdered ya see, and our cousin, Luke, he said Mr. Conover could help."

Rebecca squeezed an eye shut, "Luke, I want to say, Benson?"

"That's him." Joyce came back up the steps.

"I remember him. Speedway bomber blew his legs off."

Joyce said, "After that Luke didn't think anything'd make him happy, but Mr. Conover catching the bomber, that helped."

Rebecca nodded. Doug would've been happy to hear that. He loved helping people. So much so, depending on the case, he practically worked for free. She loved him for that even when it annoyed her; even though it left her near penniless. Word gets around all the stray dogs come looking for a handout.

"Did Mr. Conover have a partner?" Joyce asked, "Someone I could hire?"

"Yeah, me." Responding to a skeptical look, Rebecca said, "Doug and I used to work for a P.I. in Gary. Then we came here to start out own business."

A half-truth, but not a whole lie. Rebecca stirred her drink with a finger. No sense telling a stranger the whole story; how the past caught up to them and killed Doug in an alley last winter.

She stepped away, leaving the door open, gesturing for Joyce to follow her inside. The two went into the living room. Rebecca offered her the only chair still in the house. Joyce sat, but declined a drink. Then Rebecca asked for the details.

* * *

Standing in the parking lot Rebecca eyed the fast food joint. Like similar spots, the Burger Chef on Crawfordsville Road used a garish sign to distract from its banal nature. Bright red belied the assembly line inside, a beige factory cranking out burgers. The way customers streamed in and out, she found it hard to imagine anything grim ever happened here.

According to Joyce, her brother David, Molly Simpson, and Pete and Liz Friedmont vanished around midnight on November 17, 1978. Two days later a hiker stumbled on them in a wooded field in nearby Johnson County. The police assumed a robbery gone wrong, investigated a bit, but eventually gave up.

A beat up Ford Cortina shivered into the parking lot. Rebecca waved, and the driver parked close. Out stepped a bearded man in a coffee stained shirt.

He introduced himself, "George Smith, Speedway Town Press."

"I know. I'm the one who called you," Rebecca shook his hand.

"Ope, I'm sorry. When you mentioned a private investigation, I assumed a man'd be here."

Rebecca pointed at the Burger Chef, "What happened

here?”

“A tragedy. I mean, nothing gets the ink flowing like blood, but they didn’t even get to own the front page, had to share it with that Jonestown mess. But yeah…” George trailed off.

Rebecca gestured for him to go on. He continued like a camp counselor reciting a ghost story. She tried not to roll her eyes. Every little bit helped, and reporters often possessed grim pieces the police don’t make public. Like how the knife broke off in one of the teens, and another, trying to run away, slammed into a tree so hard he ended up drowning in his own blood.

He must’ve been really bolting Rebecca thought, though her mind orbited the knife. It takes a serious thrust to break a blade. They didn’t even stab Doug that severely.

George said, “Two of the teens got shot execution style.”

“Just the two?”

“Yep.” George plucked a small notepad out of a back pocket, “You think that means anything?”

Rebecca said, “How much did the robbers get?”

George replied, “They took $581, but left hundreds in change.”

Rebecca raised an eyebrow. According to George, the cops figured one of the teenagers recognized the robbers. That sealed their fate.

“What’s the last thing they did?”

George scratched his beard, “One of ‘em was taking out the trash. That’s the last thing anybody knows for sure.”

Rebecca headed around back. George called after her, feeling it necessary to mention the crime happened six months ago. She ignored him because she already knew. Not that she read about it at the time. Doug’s death distracted her back then. When she climbed out of the coffin beside him, the news cycle had moved on to more recent tragedies.

Behind the Burger Chef she found what she expected. The usual dumpster smelling of rot. A galaxy of cigarette butts littered the ground around it, along with a few last burnt bits of joints. She picked up a roach, sniffed it. The remnant smelled like quality product.

Catching up to her George remarked, “Like I said, this all happened six months ago. I don’t know what you expect to find.”

However, Rebecca didn’t look at the restaurant. She looked out at the surrounding area. She considered how she’d rob this place. She headed to the nearby alley.

Meanwhile, George asked, “So, who hired you? I assume

it's a victim's family."

Rebecca replied, "Assume away."

She turned back to face the Burger Chef. It made sense. Someone waited for the trash to be taken out then rushed the unlocked door. Maybe they even put a gun to whichever employee came out. However, that made things even stranger because it meant someone knew the routine. A planned robbery that left money behind struck her as more than odd.

She said, "Do the police think it was an opportunistic crime? Drunks or junkies rolling some spot."

George said, "Maybe you should ask them."

Rebecca frowned, "Joyce Caruthers hired me."

"Ah ha." George didn't write anything down, "She's a pretty girl. Works over at a resort in Roselawn. Nudist resort." He wiggled his eyebrows.

That actually inspired a question, "Two of the victims were women. Were they assaulted, sexually?"

George shook his head, "Nope which isn't to say they were virgins either. At least not Molly Simpson."

Word on the street amounted to her being willing to go with anyone in a leather jacket. Rebels on motorcycles always caught her eye. The police questioned her most recent boyfriends. Each owned an airtight alibi.

"Honestly, I don't think this is ever going to get solved," George said.

Rebecca looked at him, "Then why're you here?"

"Slow news week."

She frowned.

George added, "I mean, we could've done this over the phone, but I wanted to meet the investigator. For the story."

She started back towards Crawfordsville Road. George followed her, rambling something about a nearby cop bar. If she wanted to get a drink, they could wait there for a few police to get off work; he'd help her ask questions.

"What do you say?" George asked, "First round is on me."

He smiled. She looked up and down the street. A few businesses dotted the sides of the road. Each seemed easier to rob than a stray burger joint. It seemed to her that made Burger Chef a conscious choice.

A lone pickup rattled by, a thin cloud of rust flying off behind it. The street struck her as a road to nowhere. The suburban sprawl peppering it just made that impression worse. Doug wouldn't've agreed. He'd find the beauty in it.

"So, how about a drink?" George said.

She said, "I have work to do."

He held up his hands, "If you change your mind, Indie Rose, that's where I'll be."

She watched him drive away. Then she got into a Buick Electra, borrowed from a neighbor, and consulted her notes. Joyce provided a few addresses, victims' friends and family. The police probably interviewed them, but Rebecca knew not everyone tells the cops the whole truth.

* * *

Mary Higgins asked if she could bum a smoke. Rebecca passed the teenager one. Mary declined the lighter and pulled out her own. As she puffed, she glanced around.

"If my folks see me, I'm dead," Mary said.

Rebecca nodded. She figured that must've been part of the reason Mary insisted they go for a walk. Lying to Mom and Pop Higgins about a need for privacy gave the teen an excuse to smoke; steady her nerves while thinking about the murder.

Mary said, "I haven't seen any of the photos or anything, but like, I have nightmares sometimes about what happened."

Rebecca understood. She knew too much about what happened to Doug. She didn't even have to be asleep to have her imagination torture her with images — face smashed by a brick; stabbed seven times.

Rebecca said, "Did you know the victims?"

Mary bobbed her head side to side, "Only David and Liz. Pete and Molly, I'd say hi, but I didn't hang out with them."

Wind rustled leaves in the trees. It almost sounded like someone saying shush.

"Was David a nervous person? Did he frighten easily?" Rebecca asked.

Mary shook her head. She described David the way someone depicts a white knight in a fairy tale. That he stood up to bullies in their high school. He didn't always win fights, but he never shied away from them. Rebecca wondered then what caused him to run so fast he wrecked himself on a tree. However, she didn't share such thoughts with Mary.

The young lady looked like a stack of cards. Milk white in an unhealthy way she seemed about to crumble. Her hands trembled, unsettled by thoughts of the killing. So, Rebecca tried to steer Mary's thoughts with questions meant to keep her from colliding with any hazardous notions.

"The police thought Molly's boyfriend might be a

suspect."

"You mean boyfriends. It's hard to get a date because Molly Simpson is banging everyone." Mary grimaced, "I shouldn't say that. She was nice. She was easy, but not like slutty, do you know what I mean?"

"I think so," Rebecca said, "But did her boyfriends treat her nice?"

"I guess. Like I said, we weren't friends, but if someone was treating her bad, her brother, Chad, he'd've messed them up."

Rebecca made a mental note. A protective brother might have his own list of suspects.

She asked, "What's Chad like?"

"He's creepy as hell. He was in Vietnam, so ya know. He didn't come back right."

"Did you tell the police that?"

Mary shook her head. Her eyes seemed to lose their shine. She apologized and pulled out a small metal box. Opening it, she plucked a pill from a stash.

Popping it in her mouth she said, "I find it so hard to relax these days. I keep thinking how easy it is for people to disappear and die."

Rebecca understood. Doug went out for groceries. He promised to bring back ice cream. They were going to cozy up on the couch and watch *All Quiet on the Western Front*. Doug loved Hemingway. Instead, he died in an alley.

Rebecca said, "Why do I get the feeling those aren't from a doctor?"

"Because they aren't."

"Where'd you get them?"

Mary stopped. She dropped her cigarette. Stamping it out she shrugged.

Rebecca said, "I need a refill."

Mary hesitated then said, "There's a lot of places in town."

"Where's the best spot?"

"It depends on what you want."

Mary started walking again. She seemed better. Chemical confidence carrying her along.

Mary chuckled, "Funny thing is, the Burger Chef actually used to be the best. That's where everybody got their weed until…" she trailed off. A tear dripped out one eye. She shook it off, "But things change, ya know?"

"I do," Rebecca said, trying not to think about Doug, "I get the feeling after what happened, the dealers stopped using that spot."

Nodding Mary added, "That and they lost Pete. He only worked there to sell weed. He was going places that way, you know what I mean?"

* * *

Flashing lights in the rearview. Rebecca swore. She pulled over. Getting her license and registration ready she heard several doors close. Glancing in the mirror she saw four cops approaching the car. She locked her door.

Rolling the window down a crack, she waited for the cops to come close.

A beer bellied officer rapped on the glass, "Ma'am, I'm gonna need you to roll the window down. All the way."

Rebecca said, "It's broke. That's as far as it goes."

The officer frowned, "Ma'am, don't make me repeat myself."

"You heard me the first time."

The two glared at one another. She heard the crunch of gravel, guessed at cops skulking around the back. Yet, Rebecca kept her eyes locked on the bison before her.

Hooking thumbs into belt loops he said, "You know the routine?"

She passed the paperwork through the crack. He waved it off. Her reputation somehow proceeded her. She guessed the reporter produced that newsflash.

Rebecca said, "This the hard talk?"

"Only as hard as you make it."

She nodded.

The cop went on, "This Burger Chef business, it's a real shame, but the thing is, when there's no one to haul in, bring to justice so to speak, people prefer to forget."

"And that's not easy with someone asking questions," a gruff voice spoke up.

Rebecca glanced at the side view. She saw a tall officer standing by her bumper. When he saw her eying him, he shined a flashlight at the mirror, blinding her briefly.

Rebecca said, "I called on some families, a few friends, but not everyone talked to me."

Beer belly asked, "Who talked to you?"

"No one you didn't already."

He leaned against the door, causing the whole car to dip down, "Sounds like you didn't get much more than we did, and we couldn't figure this out, so..."

Rebecca forced a smile, "That's the end of things."

"Good to know we're on the same page."

The officer gave the roof a solid slap. He whistled. She heard the crunch of gravel. Checking the mirrors, she watched the cops return to their cruiser.

One of them got on the loudspeaker, "You can go now."

She pulled away. However, instead of heading home she casually drove out of sight. Then she piloted the Electra to the bar George mentioned.

* * *

Rebecca entered Indie Rose. The place looked like the kind of dive people spit on the floor and no one complains. The smell of beer barely masked the stench of failure. A row of sweaty barflies buzzed at the bar. Idle banter stoked worn out opinions — "I'm telling you that hick from French Lick is gonna be a star."

Several glanced over to appraise the new arrival. Some wolves licked their lips.

The bartender asked, "What can I do for you?"

Rebecca said, "I'm looking for George Smith."

The bartender pointed towards the back. Heading in that direction, Rebecca noticed an intermittent clickety-clack. It grew louder the closer she got. Coming around the booth she found George hammering away at a Selectric typewriter.

"The great American novel?" she remarked taking a seat opposite.

George smirked, "Maybe. Folks loved *In Cold Blood*." He downed a scotch, "Didn't expect to see you again."

"Why? Because you sicced the cops on me."

"Slander!" He ripped out the page and inserted a fresh blank, "But if I did, although clever, that'd be very petty of me."

Rebecca lit a cigarette. She let the lighter keep burning. Touching a flame to the edge of George's manuscript, she wondered how long until he noticed the pile burning. Fire ate a corner before he swatted frantically to save his pages.

Rebecca snapped her lighter shut.

George stood. She did the same.

He advanced on her growling, "Crazy bitch."

She kicked him between the legs. Professional kickers punt with less force. As he doubled over in pain, his legs going rubbery, George started to fall forward. Rebecca grabbed him by the ear and used his downward momentum to slam his head into the table. The reporter bounced off hard, hit the floor even harder, and began rolling around, moaning in agony.

Leaning back against the table, Rebecca said, "Now, to satisfy my curiosity, did the cops do you a favor, scaring the skirt that turned you down, or did they have their own interest in coming after me?"

George groaned, "I don't know what you're talking about."

Rebecca threaded the cigarette between her lips. She lifted the typewriter off the table. Then she slammed it down on George's side.

A chuckle drifted over from the bar.

Rebecca said, "You want to try that again?"

"Allen Taylor! He's a cop. He was sticking it to Molly Simpson."

Rebecca said, "Let me guess. He's a tall fellow, got a family and a reputation to protect."

George sat up, "Yeah, yeah, plus he's thirty, she was sixteen." George winced, "No way it would've looked good."

But the boys in blue never really investigated one of their own. They might ask Allen if he did it, though they'd take him at his word. They always did. She used to trust cops. Doug showed her enough to never make that mistake again. Still, killing four people to hide a Lolita love affair seemed excessive. Though one lead sometimes leads to another. She taught Doug that.

As such, this thread inspired her to asked, "Any chance Chad knew about Taylor?"

George sighed, "Why don't you ask him yourself?"

"Good idea. Where can I find him?"

A moldy woman at the bar called over, "Hey sweetie, he works at Allison Transmission. Go now you'll get there when he gets off."

Rebecca thanked her as she strolled out. Not everyone in this town seemed terrible. Just the folks trying to appear respectable.

* * *

Driving through the city, Rebecca kept wondering whether it changed, or her eyes had. She used to remember kids coming home when the streetlights went on, parents trusting the children to know it isn't safe after dark. Now, parents stood on front steps shouting for kids to come home. No one willing to risk the bogeymen they could no longer deny. It already snatched four teens from the Burger Chef.

As she pulled into the parking lot for Allison Transmission, Rebecca parked in front of a group of guys smoking around a Firebird. She rolled down her window.

Seeing her, one shouted, "Hey baby, you looking for fun? I'm the ride of a lifetime."

She said, "You guys know Chad Simpson?"

The lascivious expressions vanished from their faces.

The one who shouted asked, "You Chad's lady?"

"Maybe," Rebecca said.

"Hey, I didn't mean nothing."

"You know what? Tell me where he's at, he won't hear a thing about it."

The shouter gave her directions, adding, "You ain't gonna tell Chad?"

Rebecca winked, and drove off. She chuckled thinking about how much Doug loved that gambit. They called it the catcall con, and it offered up myriad avenues. Then thoughts twisted to Doug in that goddamn alley. Did he think about her towards the end, maybe even blame her for it? She tried to imagine him in the passenger seat saying, "Honey, don't mind that horseshit," but she kept envisioning him covered in blood, his face caved in by a brick, torso full of bloody wells pouring like Niagara.

She snapped on the radio. Hot Chocolate's "Everyone 1's a Winner" started playing. Rebecca bobbed her head, doing her best to ignore the dark thoughts crowding in as the streetlights came on.

* * *

A single red dot glowed on the porch steps. Someone, who knows when, destroyed all the lamps on the street. That single red comet briefly flared, vaguely illuminating a harsh face.

Parking, Rebecca assessed the situation. Caution dictated taking the Beretta out of the glove compartment. Doug would. She figured otherwise. Although folks obviously feared Chad, none of them ever shared a specific example. The threat of him more implied than proven. However, the one-time Doug went out with no weapon, he ended up in the ground.

She put the pistol in her coat pocket. She approached slowly, making as much noise as possible. Rebecca didn't want Chad to think she tried sneaking up on him.

She saw the red dot shift, moved as a head turned in her direction. When she got close enough Rebecca waved.

She said, "Chad?"

"Who're you?" his voice sounded like death.

She introduced herself. No secrets. She laid out her presence and purpose plain.

Chad sighed, "Lemme guess, fingers are pointing my way."

Rebecca said, "If your sister wasn't dead, I'd say maybe they're right, but she is, so I'm not inclined that way."

He stood. Nonchalantly as possible, she took hold of the pistol, but kept it in her pocket. Chad turned. He went inside, leaving the door open behind him. Rebecca followed.

Inside amounted to even less light. For a moment, she suspected having made a mistake. Then a light snapped on. Yet, shadows still reigned.

Chad filled a glass with whiskey. He downed it and held up the bottle.

Recognizing an offer, Rebecca accepted. Chad fetched a glass from the kitchen. Returning with it full, he sat down at a scarred wooden table. Chewed up by nails and knives, Rebecca suspected it bore the brunt of many sleeplessness nights. Now that she could see him in the light, Chad looked like a caged tiger — something sad yet dangerous.

Chad said, "What do you wanna know?"

Rebecca sat across from him. At first, they went over the details of the crime. She wanted to see what he knew and how he reacted. Six months is a long time to get used to feelings, but not if any guilt lingers. Doug taught her that. Even the absence of feelings can be telling. She taught him that.

Eventually Rebecca asked, "What did you think of your sister's boyfriends?"

Chad snorted, "Assholes. Every single one, but hey, not like I dated alotta winners either."

Rebeca said, "Did you think any of them might've..."

"Nope," he cut in, "If I did, they wouldn't be around, you can be sure of that."

"What about Allen Taylor?"

Chad cocked an eyebrow, "You know about him?"

"I'm good at this."

He nodded then told a story. How right about when cops started saying they'd let the case go cold, Chad heard a rumor. He went to ask Taylor about it.

Chad said, "So I bust into his kitchen, wait for him to wake up." Chad snickered, "Hell, I'm also sobering up, so I don't do anything stupid, but he comes in, and we get to chatting." — refilling their glasses — "He almost pissed himself when he saw me."

Rebecca chuckled. Chad smiled. Doug would've liked

him. She downed her whiskey.

Chad went on, "Allen hasn't got the balls to kill one person, forget about four."

Rebecca said, "You got any ideas on who did it?"

Scratching at the table, Chad said, "Whoever it is, they're local, or else how'd they think to go to Johnson County?"

That sparked a notion, "Does anyone live in those woods?"

"Nah, not really, but they will. Believe me. It's too pretty to be left alone." He chuckled.

"What?"

"It's nothing." He scraped a fresh line into the table with his finger, "There's always someone out there. I'm sure it'll be homes one day."

Rebecca probed, "What kind of people?"

Chad leaned back, "Folks like Ronnie Brooks. He's this guy sells shitty weed to whoever doesn't know better, mostly high school kids."

Following the thread, Rebecca said, "What's he do out there?"

Chad shrugged, "He shoots paint cans with this .38 that always jams. Says it's for anyone who screws him."

"Anybody ever screw him over?"

Chad shook his head, "Anyone could, but he's too stupid to be anything except mean. It would end bad."

* * *

Ronnie Brooks lived in the kind of house that inspired urban legends. A sagging mass of timber wondering about death's delay. According to Chad, anyone who complained about Ronnie to his face got bricks through windows and murdered pets.

Rebecca circled the block a few times before parking. She saw a bit of light through the pulled curtains. Pocketing her gun, she got out.

Heading towards the house she knitted threads. After drinks with Chad she went home. The next afternoon she made a few phone calls. Mary Higgins led her to Daniel Krueger, who steered her to Lucy Pendleton, so on and so forth until Rebecca harvested enough from the grapevine to get the picture.

Rebecca knew teens aren't likely to volunteer information about their drug buying habits, especially not to cops. Add on the fact that once the blue boys' buddy, Allen Taylor, entered the equation, they started avoiding details to help the case grow cold. A perfect storm of everybody not wanting to get noticed doing the wrong thing blinded every eye to potential threads.

It seemed Pete Friedmont aspired to be a drug pusher. At the very least, he dabbled in the trade, often aiming for a big score — get rich quick mentality. Shortly before the murders he mentioned to a few friends he came into a stash of cash.

Lucy Pendleton said, "I remember him saying he got his hands on a lot of money, and that he'd never worry about paying it back."

Rebecca asked, "Why not?"

"Because the guy he got it from was some loser idiot or something."

Rebecca, a hand on her gun, knocked on Ronnie's door. She heard stirring within. A nearby curtain flashed aside. She saw the face of a gargoyle for a moment. The curtain flapped shut. Moments later the door opened.

Ronnie Brooks smelled like wet dog. His clothes didn't seem like they'd survive another wash cycle if they ever saw one.

He grunted, "What?"

Rebecca said, "Did you know Pete Friedmont?"

Ronnie folded his arms across his chest, "Who the hell are you?"

"I'm a friend of Chad Simpson."

He snorted, "That supposed to scare me?"

Doug sometimes said don't poke the bear in the zoo. Solid advice except lately, Rebecca felt like jamming a thumb in the animal's eye.

She said, "I know."

He let loose a rusty chuckle.

Shaking his head Ronnie said, "What're you talking about?"

Rebecca said, "I know Pete Friedmont screwed you on a drug deal. That you went to go teach him a lesson, and being the badass pet killer you are, you probably smacked his sister around a bit. Either way, along comes David Caruthers, knight in shining armor. He doesn't win the fight, but things are getting out of hand, and everyone knows who you are. So..."

"So what?" Ronnie glared at her. She could feel the hate in his gaze like smoldering coals.

Unflinching, Rebecca said, "So you did something stupid because that's what idiots do."

She didn't even see him move. Ronnie backhanded her across the face, smacking her off the porch. Rebecca tumbled down the steps. She heard him stomping down after her. Springing to her feet, Rebecca pulled out the gun. She pointed it right at Ronnie's face.

He sneered, "Who're you kidding?"

She cocked the hammer back. His expression changed. The rage remained, yet a doubt now existed.

Rebecca backed away, holding the gun steady. Ronnie didn't follow. She kept an eye on him all the way back to her car. He watched her drive away.

Six blocks along she imagined bloody Doug in the passenger seat.

He asked, "What'd you expect to happen?"

"I don't know," she lied. She wanted the killer to be a killer.

She spent the rest of the drive waiting for the ghost to bite, but he never did. Back home, Rebecca poured four fingers of vodka. She started considering a plan, some way to investigate. The phone rang.

She answered, "Hello?"

"Hey, it's Chad. You left me this number in case I thought of anything else."

"Did you?"

He said, "No, but I just heard from a buddy, Ronnie Brooks is spitting mad. He's bar hopping looking for me and my bitch?"

Rebecca sighed. She didn't know if she should admit everything. Her supposition amounted to a shot in the dark. Nothing made it truer than any other guess. Yet, she knew what it felt like to think justice would never come. Hell, she knew who killed Doug, but some folks are beyond that proverbial long arm of the law, especially when it won't reach for them. So, she told Chad what she thought happened.

When she finished, he said, "I see..." mumbled a few words then he hung up.

Rebecca closed her eyes and drained the bottle. A week later a letter from Chad arrived.

It read, "In Ronnie's basement I found a Burger Chef hat like Eve Plumb wore in those commercials. Molly got killed in her uniform. Pretty sure it's hers."

It didn't say much else. It didn't need to. After reading it, Rebecca phoned Joyce to let her know a kind of justice prevailed. Doug might've worried it wasn't the best kind, but Rebecca figured it was better than nothing.

J. Rohr is a Chicago native with a taste for history and wandering the city at odd hours. In order to deal with the more corrosive aspects of everyday life he writes the blog www.honestyisnotcontagious.com and makes music in the band Beerfinger. His Twitter babble can be found @JackBlankHSH.

It All Comes Out in The Wash

By N. B. Turner

The washer came to life with a sound like a gunshot. My sweaty palms dragged across my thighs as I sat down on a plastic stool in the mudroom.

My husband's old boots stood straight up by the door. His coat hung on the wall hook, sweat-stained ball cap inside the pocket. His blood stained the white dress slapping around inside the washer. His body was dissolving in our bathroom.

I hoped I used enough bleach in the wash. This bottle was all I had left.

The blue and white bottle shook with the washer, cap shifting left and right like a metronome. My heart pounded in time with the bottle. The room was hot and my skin slick with sweat. Ridges from the stool pressed into my ass as I started to squirm. I twisted my wedding band around my finger. The gold looked dull under the light. Didn't even have a diamond I could pawn. I flicked it over my shoulder like a worthless coin.

* * *

My husband wasn't a bad man. He was just the wrong man for me. He took up too much space in our bed and too little in my heart. A young, beautiful boy was enough to shake him loose.

The boy's arms were slim. That was the first thing I saw. Muscle in them for sure, but not bulky hammer-swinging muscle. And his eyes—those blue eyes shined in the dim light, like a flashlight at the top of a dark well. Eyes like those make you think you can be saved.

Behind the bar, I served his beers and asked the questions bartenders ask. Nothing threatening. Nothing prying. You let them know that you're here if they need anything. When they call you back over, then you can start flirting.

When he called me, his eyes looked lonely, like he was hoping for someone to be with. "You're very pretty," he said. He looked at me as he spoke, then looked away. He looked like a college kid, maybe from South Bend. Not a Domer. They'd never come out to the sticks.

"Glad to hear that from a handsome boy like you," I said. I threw him a wink when no one was watching. The boy's eyes drifted to my chest and then to my hand.

"You married?" he said, tilting his bottle back.

"No." I slipped the ring to my right hand. "It's an heirloom from my grandmother." He smiled and shifted his eyes to my chest again. Then to my face. Got him.

The boy tipped well enough to make up for a shitty shift. He asked when I'd be working again. I told him, and he showed up. Every time I saw him, I slipped my ring to my right hand. The only mistake was the one time I forgot to switch it back when I came home. That was the only time my husband hit me. Didn't keep me from wanting the boy in my bed.

* * *

The bleach bottle clattered to the floor and knocked into a half-filled jar of change. Coins rattled against the glass, but the jar stayed standing. Washing the dress was taking forever.

I padded towards the bathroom where I'd left my husband. He was wasting away, not feeling the chemicals soak through his skin. Hopefully he wasn't. I didn't want him to suffer. Didn't want him to hurt. Just wanted him out of my life. He wouldn't go otherwise.

* * *

I asked him one night if he was happy.

"What kind of weird question is that?"

"My kind of weird question." I snuggled close to him in bed, trying to be cute, hoping to flirt or weasel an answer out of him.

"Then, yeah, sure."

"You don't sound happy."

"Should I do a dance or something? Why don't you believe me?"

"Because you don't sound convincing."

"Do you need convinced? I'm going to be here, no matter what. Do you think I'd leave just because I wasn't happy?"

I didn't answer. I was afraid. Afraid that he wouldn't leave. He was stubborn enough to stay even if he was miserable. The bastard.

* * *

The washer buzzed when I came back to the mudroom. Next part of the cycle. How much blood was left on the dress? How much of him was left behind on me?

It was supposed to be easy. The kitchen had plenty of knives. A search on the library computer told me that the taxidermy chemicals my husband used to clean animal bones were good for humans too. Just needed a bit of safety gear. A plastic tub, a bit of plastic wrap that my husband for his dead deer, and a bit of time, I could dump the body in a hole out back. An afternoon of work and I'd be free. No divorce needed.

I waited for a day that I was off at the bar. I needed to make sure no one would miss me. I texted my husband around the time he normally got off work: *'Hey baby, when you coming back?"*

"Getting off work now. Why?"

"Just thinking about you. Here by myself. Wearing that white dress you love. Hoping I don't have to be alone for too much longer."

"Thinking about me?"

"Well, parts of you anyway. ;)"

"I'll be home ASAP."

So many things I was taught as a kid fell through as I got older: my husband's desire for sex was not one of them. I was warned by my mother, by the boys at the church I'd left, that men are insatiable. My husband proved them right.

I pulled on my white linen dress and waited in the kitchen for him.

He came through the mudroom door and called for me.

"In here, darling!"

The kitchen was right beside the mudroom. He shot around the corner in his socks. I stood by the knives, curling my finger to call him to me. "You beautiful baby…" he whispered. He ran to me, kissed me, slipping his tongue past my teeth. Cigarettes and mint gum. His rough hands moved slowly on my chest. They always did.

He moved to remove my panties but found nothing. His hands around my hips, I reached back for a knife. His eyes were closed. Mine were open. The knife stuck in his neck like a joystick: I could have controlled him like a puppet.

His mouth moved without a sound. "Don't ask why," I said. I pulled the knife out and pushed him away from me. He fell to the floor, unable to catch himself. He tried to roll to his stomach, but I grabbed his neck to stop him. My small hand rolled him to

71

his back. The knife pierced through his eye. He stopped moving.

Blood everywhere. He didn't land on the plastic wrap I'd put nearby. Son of a bitch, making me bring out the rags and Lysol. I dragged him onto the plastic and then dragged the plastic towards the bathroom. Red streaked the floor as we moved. More shit to clean.

My bloody hands couldn't keep a grip on the plastic. By habit, I wiped them on my dress. It didn't help. Red had soaked through the white. I wiped my hands on a dry portion of my legs and grabbed the plastic again.

I tilted the long blue Rubbermaid tub on its side to shove him inside. A pain shot through my back as I pushed it upright. "You heavy son of a bitch," I told him. His feet stuck over the end of the box.

"Of course you would make me cut you up," I said. *Why am I talking to a dead man?* I thought.

A hacksaw and hammer from the garage took care of his feet. His ankles broke with a strange noise: a violent *pop*, not a *crack,* muffled by the towel I wrapped around them before I used the hammer. Broken bones made sawing through his skin easier. I tossed his feet in with the rest of his body and poured in the chemicals.

It took three buckets of bleach and water, rubber gloves, and enough scrubbing to turn my knees raw before I got all the blood off the floor. I burned the paper towels and rags in the garage.

I needed a shower, and to finish what my husband started. Hurts when you get excited but can't get your rocks off.

* * *

The washer ground to a stop. I opened it hopeful and closed it pissed off. The dress still had splotches of blood on it. "Fuck." I needed more bleach.

I peeped into the bathroom. The chemicals weren't working as fast as I thought. His shirt was just starting to slip off him after six hours in the dissolving bath. I wanted nothing solid in the ground.

The sun was down when I went outside. Clouds were forming across the level ground and a distant rumble warned of a storm. I drove to the Walmart on State Road 2 in my shorts and a tank top. Humid air fastened the cloth to my skin even with the AC blasting. Sweat on my palms kept my grip loose on the wheel. Damn humidity. Or nerves.

I hadn't expected to leave the house with his body still

dissolving. *What if someone looks in on the house? Or breaks in and finds the body?* I sped down the empty road to Walmart.

Walking into the store, I saw the security camera hovering above the door. The huge store seemed small. Every black dot on the ceiling was an eyeball searching for my face. Every person was someone the police could talk to later. And any sort of odd behavior was something that people would talk about. Indiana is a big state full of small towns, and there's no privacy in a small town.

I got the bleach and made a beeline for the register. The cashier looked as tired as I felt. "Cash or credit?" she said.

I opened my wallet and saw no cash. "Credit," I said. *Damn it,* I thought.

"Late night laundry?" cashier asked. The skin around her mouth and fingertips looked yellow. Smoker. Made me want to pick the habit up again.

"Yeah. And can I get some Camel menthols and a lighter?"

She threw them on the counter and rang them up.

I dropped the card as I tried to insert it into the machine. "Nervous about something?" she said.

"Nah. Just tired." *Stop talking, you idiot. Stop giving her reasons to remember you.*

"Well, hope everything comes out clean in the end."

"What?"

"Your laundry."

"Oh yeah. Let's hope."

I started the washing machine as soon as I could, pouring twice the usual amount over the dress. My husband was still in the plastic tub. No change from before. The bastard wouldn't leave.

The light in the kitchen never seemed bright enough at night. Shadows creep from every corner. I propped myself near the block of knives and pulled a cigarette from the pack. One drag and I wondered why I stopped smoking in the first place. Was it for my husband? Did I want to live longer for him? To grow old with him? No sense in that now. I pulled deep and held the smoke for a minute.

His face came as I rubbed my eyes, cigarette heat burning against my forehead. He looked so scared after I plunged the knife in. Big eyes and silent mouth, like a fish dying out of the water. An apology crept into my throat but didn't make it past my teeth.

I opened my eyes and was alone. Except for his body which refused to dissolve.

I fell asleep before the washer finished running. The next day, the dress still had small red dots littering the white. One more cycle of bleach as I showered.

My husband scared me when I walked into the bathroom: a large jagged shape in the darkness, it looked even worse in the light. Some skin had started to fall off. I saw pieces of bone underneath. "Hurry up, you bastard." I hopped into the shower, trying to forget he was there.

The beautiful boy came to mind as the water caressed me. Those eyes, his arms. I never felt his hands. I hoped they were knew what they were doing. If they didn't, I'd teach him. I know what I like. I'd make sure he gives it to me.

God, even thinking about it drove me nuts. I wasn't alone, but I didn't care if my husband heard. I played it up, screaming louder as I jerked off. "You like hearing that, you piece of shit?" I wanted him to know that someone I'd never had was better than he was.

"You better be gone by tonight," I told my husband before leaving the house.

The bar starts quiet. Lunchtime folks are quiet. Evening comes around and the happy hour crowd gets a little rowdy. After that, you find the serious drinkers. The boy came in during the happy hour and stayed. "Where's your ring?" he said.

"Just didn't feel like wearing it today," I said. He didn't argue.

He drank slowly, like he was waiting for something. Two drinks an hour, but he stuck around until last call. He tried to flirt as best as a shy boy could. "You waiting for something?"

"Wondering if you'd want to come with me after your shift," he said. Finally.

I played innocent. "Come where?"

"My car."

"You want to fuck in your car?"

He shrugged.

"No way. If we're going to fuck, we're going to a house."

"Your house?"

"Why not yours?"

"You want to drive 45 minutes away?" *Shit. This wasn't part of the plan. I was hoping he lived closer.*

"Not tonight. Tomorrow."

"Why not tonight?"

"I want to make it good for you."

"Then tomorrow night."

"Best get driving home then. Get rested."

"Yes, ma'am."

He stood up and paid his tab. No one else was here. "Hey, kid." I kissed him. "Call it a down payment." He smiled, those blue eyes flashing.

Back at home, my husband was nowhere near dissolved. Chunks of flesh floated in the tub. It was starting to overflow the rim. I couldn't wait until he was done. He had to go now.

I poured the liquid into the bathtub, watching it swirl down the drain. Only a bunch of disconnected flesh and bones remained. Rubber gloves on, I picked up a bone. It snapped like a twig. This was doable. I just needed a hole, some more plastic, and a large bucket.

Digging the hole was awful. The ground was heavy and sopping wet. Rain had soaked it through the night I killed him.

I dug the hole behind the treeline of our property, hiding from neighborly eyes. I dug fast, thinking the night was speeding to dawn. I dug and dug until the hole was too deep for him to come up. This was supposed to be easy. Easy, my ass.

By the time my plastic-wrapped husband was in the ground, and all his mess was cleaned up, it was almost dawn. Stripping off my sweat-drenched clothes, I felt like a newborn: naked, covered in filth, and hating the light in my eyes. I showered and collapsed onto my bed, hoping for a few hours of sleep before I went into work.

The next day went according to plan. The boy showed up, drank, and came home with me. His car took a spot in the driveway right next to our old truck. I took him through the back door to the mudroom. My neighbors had a nasty habit of glancing at my front door at the worst times.

"Whose boots are those?" he asked, pointing to my husband's things by the door.

"Not sure. Think my brother left them here or something."

"Left his boots?"

"He's a drunk. He forgets things." I kissed him to stop his questions. Beer and cigarettes on his tongue, tinged with mint gum. Like my husband. I threw his coat off his shoulders. His hands started tugging at my shirt. "Bed's this way."

He pushed his shoes off his feet as I led him through the kitchen. I pulled him close. His stocking feet slipped and he fell back, pulling me with him. Close enough to the bed. My mouth worked from his lips to his neck. I hated the taste of his breath. My hand worked his jeans. His hands worked their way up my back, unhooking my bra. He was doing fine. I slipped everything off and pulled off his jeans.

"What's that smell?" he said.

"What smell?" *Move faster,* I thought. *Don't let him think.*

"Smells like…bleach. Why does your floor smell like bleach?"

"I cleaned it with bleach."

"It's strong. Can we move to the bed?"

"Take your socks off." He did as told. I ran to the bedroom.

We kept up the antics until he asked for a condom. "You didn't bring one?"

"Too excited to remember, I guess."

"In the bathroom." I pointed his way there.

"Good God, why does it smell like chlorine?"

"Just get the rubber and get back here!" *Get here and fuck me, damn it.*

"Sorry, lost my boner with that smell."

"Get over here and I'll get it back!"

"You're aggressive, ain't ya?"

"You have no idea."

I kissed him all over. I waited until he entered me to think about kissing his mouth. One shot of his breath made me regret it. But the way he moaned and swore and asked for more… I came up to push him deeper. I just needed to finish. "Oh beautiful baby…" he said.

I stopped. "What did you call me?"

"Nothing. Don't stop."

"You go on top."

He flipped me. When he closed his eyes, I saw my husband. He had looked like the boy when he was younger. I closed my eyes to hide the boy's face, but I saw my husband again, mouth moving without words. "Fuck…"

"You like that?" That growl was too close.

"Nope. Stop."

"What?"

"I said stop! Get out."

"What the fuck?"

I pushed him off the bed. "I said get out!"

"What the fuck is wrong with you?" He skulked from the bedroom, picking up his clothes on the way. "Crazy bitch…"

"Just leave."

"Fine." He went out half-dressed to his car. I threw on a robe and watched him from the door. His headlights sped into the distance, off to his college life. "Fuck…" I grabbed my smoke pack and shoved a cigarette between my lips. His voice, my husband's voice, still rang in my ears. *Beautiful baby*... The bastard wouldn't leave me.

In the mudroom, I remembered that I'd left my dress in the washer. It was over a day old, wet. I hoped there was no mildew. There wasn't. But unrolling it, I saw the red dots still littering its once-pristine white, like red sins on a soul. I shoved it back in, poured in more bleach, and started the wash cycle again.

I smoked and smoked in front of the washer, and prayed like the devil that everything would come out in the wash.

N.B. Turner is a young writer living in Virginia, but fondly remembering his roots in northern Indiana. Turner attempts to see the world for all its light and darkness with an honest eye and a good sense of humor. He considers himself a student of Ray Bradbury, Flannery O'Connor, and Graham Greene, and an admirer of Ottessa Moshfegh and John Le Carre. He will be published in a sci-fi anthology from Elephant's Bookshelf Press this fall, and has co-authored fantasy audio series that is being recorded by We are One Body Audio Theater in Pennsylvania.

The Selfie Killer

By N E Riggs

Travis's first kill was a spontaneous thing.

He stood close to the cliff edge, an insufficiently high railing behind him (because anything taller would ruin the view). Two stupid, suburban tourists who did not understand that nature was dangerous waved him over to join them in a selfie. Because reaching the top of the cliff wasn't the important part. The perfect, social media-ready picture at the top of the cliff was what mattered. Individual and couple shots were important, with perfect hair and clothes and no sign of sweat, but the proper, hard-core fitness junkies wanted groups who looked like they'd all suffered together. That was how a person got bragging rights.

So Travis and three others clumped around the couple, closer than sardines because no one had a selfie stick. They grinned together at the cell phone.

Travis had been waiting over thirty minutes for his selfie, and his patience had long since vanished. This couple had hogged the spot for ten minutes, which was far too long. Travis didn't really think about it. A well-placed elbow, a shift backwards of his foot, and a turn of his shoulders. That was all it took.

The man tumbled over the cliff edge with a scream, leaving behind his girlfriend and what turned out to be the most dramatic selfie ever taken in that spot.

A normal person would be appalled. A normal person might even turn themselves into the police. A normal person would avoid selfies and cliff edges for a long time.

Travis wanted to do it again.

If there was one thing that wasn't in short supply, it was people taking selfies. Cliff edges were harder to find, but Travis liked to hike.

The next weekend he headed elsewhere. It took him two hours to drive there, but he arrived at Turkey Run north of Terre

Haute by lunch time. The parking lot overflowed with cars, as it was a perfect day for a hike. Travis grabbed his water bottle and a snack, then hit the trail.

He considered hikers. He considered vantage points. He did not change his mind about his plan.

A few hours later, he found the perfect location and the perfect hikers. It was a group of five, from the university based on their conversation. He joined up with the group and they scaled a hill together, all jovial. At the top, they paused to take in the view and have something to drink. It only took a minute before one hiker suggested that they should all cluster together at the edge for a photo. Another hiker produced a selfie stick. They formed a clump and grinned up at the camera.

Travis stood at the left side since he wasn't really part of their group. An excessively blond and excessively muscular man posed beside him. He was young and strong and therefore stupid. He stood closer to the cliff edge than the others. He balanced on the tips of his toes to better lean close to his friends.

Some things were almost too easy. Travis planted a foot behind the young man's foot, placed a hand on his shoulder, and then moved. As the camera clicked, the young man let out a cry. He spiraled his arms and grabbed for anything to halt his momentum. Everyone else had turned at his cry, and there was nothing to stop him.

He toppled over, striking his head on an outcrop before flopping to a halt a few feet below. The group stared in horrified silence.

It was exhilarating. Travis wondered if this was how other killers felt. The thrill of the moment, the fear of being caught, the power that came with success. He wanted to feel that again.

He returned to his boring job, but it didn't crush his soul the way it usually did. Everyone sat in front of their computers, dead-eyed as they earned money for rich men. Those rich men were powerful, but Travis was more powerful still. He had a purpose now, a calling.

It was better not to return to the site of a previous kill. He crossed off Turkey Run and searched for other hiking trails. He lived surrounded by plains, so it took time to find a place with sufficient heights.

Travis thought about what would happen if someone survived the fall. "I didn't trip," they'd say. "That man knocked me over the side."

He couldn't have that. He had to be careful, about how he

picked his spot and how he picked his targets.

The next weekend he drove south to the Hoosier National Forest. He started with the trail guide at the information center, insisting that he wanted difficult trails, or at least trails that involved lots of inclines. The guide pointed out the best options, and Travis was off.

The weather wasn't as nice as last weekend, so he passed fewer people. That didn't worry Travis. He hadn't yet found a good location, so no point seeking out targets.

After a few hours of hiking, he had found two locations that he liked. He had no targets though. Damn these sedentary people, frightened away by mild inclines. Travis lingered at the second location while he ate a sandwich. A couple finally walked past. They smiled and greeted him and photographed each other.

"Would you like a picture together?" Travis asked.

They happily accepted his offer, but he couldn't barge in on them. They hadn't shared the experience together, and thus didn't want a group selfie that included him. He took the picture, handed back the phone, and watched as the couple continued on.

With a sigh, Travis walked the other direction. Even if he could attach himself to a group, he was too tired to walk the trail a second time. He found a cheap motel a few miles down the road and spent the night by himself. There was no one looking for him, no one who would wonder about him.

The next morning, he hung around the information center, subtly looking for a group that looked fit. Finally, a woman headed towards the steep trail. Travis trailed her.

The woman set a good pace, and Travis had to work to keep up. They passed the first overlook before the woman paused. She saw Travis behind her and smiled. "Nice, isn't it?"

"Yes. It gets even prettier if you keep going." He gestured towards the second overlook.

"Awesome." Without another look at him, she continued along.

A good killer would have walked alongside her, making enough conversation so that the inevitable moment of murder would come more easily. Travis wasn't good with people, and she was already ahead of him. Since he had no better idea, he walked that direction, many yards behind the woman.

She was in far better shape than him. Long, lean legs ate up the distance, only slowing a little on the inclines. Travis's thighs ached, and he thought his calves might fall off. At least he wore good shoes. Somehow, he kept the gap between them from growing wider.

The ridge came into sight. Reds, yellows, and oranges burst in the ravine alongside the trail, trees fighting one another to show off their autumn colors. The woman slowed to take in the views. Eternally grateful, Travis decreased his pace too. If he was going to keep this up, he would need to exercise more during the week.

The woman pulled out her phone to take pictures. Travis closed the gap between them. "Told you it was nice," he called as he approached.

"Yeah, totally." She threw him a quick grin, then returned to memorializing the view.

Travis stopped a few feet away from her. He didn't want to appear threatening. After a minute, he said, "You want me to take a picture of you?"

The woman grinned. "Yeah, sure." She held out her phone.

Travis accepted it. The woman took a few steps back, standing closer to the edge than she'd been before. She posed as Travis snapped pictures, her grin a mile wide. Finally, Travis lowered the phone and walked towards the woman, holding it out for her. He moved quickly, covering the distance between them before she could reach a safer perch. Her smile didn't falter. Like all his other victims, she didn't see him as a threat.

Unlike the previous times, Travis didn't stand next to the woman. In the few moments he took to reach her, she stepped away from the edge. It was still a precarious position, but not as much as Travis would have liked. His previous victims were strong, young men. The woman was further away and the angle wasn't as good, but he could overpower her. The thrill of excitement burned away any reservations.

Their hands touched as he made to pass her the phone. In that moment, Travis shifted forward. He slapped her hand wide, then planted his shoulder against her middle and pushed. The woman screamed, arms and legs flailing as she groped for purchase. Travis hooked his foot behind hers and pushed harder. Nails raked across his arm and face, but it wasn't enough.

The woman grabbed at bushes and tufts of grass. She skidded a foot, slowing as she went. That was unacceptable. She had to die. A large branch lay on the ground nearby. Travis picked it up and swung it down towards the woman.

"What--" She stared up desperately.

He smacked her across the head and the arms. She let go and fell the rest of the way.

When her scream died away, Travis stood at the edge, panting. This wasn't what he wanted. He liked to see them smile as they fell, one last, perfect picture before death. Where was the satisfaction in this?

The sense of accomplishment and power from before didn't return. Travis felt empty. When he looked at his hands and saw scratch marks, his heart skipped a beat. Before she fell, the woman clawed at him. When the authorities retrieved the body, there might be traces of his blood on her. And his fingerprints might show on the branch he beat her with.

He threw the branch away. It bounced down the ridge, until it got stuck between two rocks, not far from the woman's body. That did nothing to calm him down. The police would notice that branch when they came to investigate. Travis had to do something, before he got caught.

The woman's phone lay on the ground, dropped and forgotten during their tussle. Travis hesitated to pick it up, but he'd already touched it. It had no security code and opened immediately for him. He called the police.

"You've got to come help! A woman fell over the side of a cliff!" He didn't have to force the breathlessness into his voice. When he thought about getting caught, it came naturally. "We just met on the trail, and I took her photo, and then she just fell!"

The police promised to come quickly. They told him to stay in place and remain calm. Travis agreed and hung up.

There was no evidence of foul play. He would tell the police that he tried to save the woman, but failed. There were scuff marks in the grass, but they could be caused by a desperate rescue attempt. That could also explain Travis's scratches.

It would be fine. The police had no reason to suspect him.

Travis wiped his hands on his shirt. He should have waited for a better opportunity. He'd been too eager, too full of power from his first two kills.

How easy was it for the police to trace someone from blood samples? TV and movies made it look simple, but was it? Travis had no idea.

He could leave. Maybe the police wouldn't be able to find him. Surely it was better to flee than to stay here and wait for the police. But he'd already called the police, and his fingerprints were on the phone.

No. He could fix that.

He pulled out his water bottle. He wiped the phone on his shirt, then dumped the entire contents of the water bottle on it. That should be enough to ruin any fingerprints.

Now he could run. Maybe the woman still had a little of his blood on her nails, but that wouldn't be enough to catch him. Unlike finger prints, the police didn't keep blood samples on file. Travis was pretty sure about that.

It was safe for him to run now. He hesitated. Running away would be admitting his guilt. If the police found him, he wouldn't be able to talk his way out of it.

The thrill never came, and Travis couldn't keep still. Even if he stayed and tried to lie to the police, he didn't think he could keep it up.

So he turned to head back down the trail. A fork a mile away would take him in a different direction, help him avoid the police and any rescue teams. As long as he could get that far, he'd be fine.

His feet took over from his brain, and Travis made his way back. He moved as quickly as he dared. Though he wanted to run, that would look suspicious. Also, after hours of walking, his legs refused to move that fast, no matter how much he urged them towards greater speeds.

The trail twisted and turned, and Travis got closer to the fork. Hope bloomed inside him. He was going to make it. He would get out of here, wash the blood from his arms and face, and throw the woman's phone away in a trash miles away. The police in TV and movies could trace a person with virtually nothing, but that was fiction. In real life, they couldn't be that good. Travis would be fine. And he'd wait until a better opportunity before he tried to kill again.

The first ridge stood between him and the fork. As Travis approached it, he heard talking and laughter. His heart skipped a beat, but he told himself to stay calm. The police didn't laugh while searching for a body, and neither did rescue crews. This must be a group of hikers.

He forced himself to slow and keep his head down. He didn't want them to notice him.

"Wow! Isn't that gorgeous?" one said.

"It's a perfect view," said another.

"We need to get a picture here. Hey, you!"

Travis forced himself to look up. Six young people clustered together.

One gestured at him. "Can you take our picture?"

A smile forced its way onto Travis's face. "Of course." He held out his hand for the phone.

The group bunched up at the side of the trail, far too close to the edge. This was what he should have waited for. The woman had far more sense than this group. Travis snapped pictures as the group posed and laughed.

"Thanks, man," they said as they finally finished.

"Of course." Travis approached the group with the phone held out. The young people still stood far too close to the edge. His mind showed him many ways where he could easily knock one of them over.

He returned the phone. That person and two others moved away, but the other three stayed where they were. One leaned so far over that Travis wondered if anyone needed to push him over the edge.

"It's beautiful, isn't it?" he said.

The leaning man grinned without pulling back. "It sure is. Is it nicer up ahead?"

"Oh, yes," Travis said without thought. Then he realized what he'd done. If these people continued on and found the second ridge, they would stop and look. They would see the woman's body. At that point, they might suspect Travis. He'd just come from that direction, and he'd called the police.

He didn't panic. There was one sure way to distract police investigating a possible murder, and that was by giving them a second body. Travis already stood close to the man leaning way too far over the side.

He took a step nearer to the leaning man. He looked down, pretending to be careful of where he stepped but really looking for the best way to trip the other man.

Then he was in place, his left foot next to the leaning man's right foot. Travis also leaned out, though not as far. "It's a shame so few people come this far," he said. Most visitors kept to the lower paths.

"That's so true, man," said the leaning man.

Travis made his move. At the same time, someone else in the group called out, "Come on!"

The leaning man turned to look around. Travis's foot got caught up in his, and he tripped. The world spun, and Travis pinwheeled his arms, trying to find his balance. Someone shouted something, and a hand reached for Travis.

He could still do this. It would work out better this way, to kill the person who tried to rescue him. No one would suspect foul play. Travis kicked out a foot and pushed at the arm.

The world tilted again, worse than before. The woman's

phone slipped from his pocket and flew past his line of vision. The sky twisted, and Travis saw the far side of the ridge, upside down. Air whistled past, and he realized that he was falling. The hikers stared down at him, horror written on their faces.

Travis craned his neck and had one glance at the huge boulder below. Anger filled him, but there was nothing he could do about it. For a brief time, he had power. That power was gone now.

His head struck the boulder, and there was nothing.

N E Riggs is from Chicago and currently lives in Vincennes, Indiana. N E is a math professor and martial artist who likes to combine fantasy and science fiction elements in new and weird ways. N E has published three series: Tomb of the Moon is book 1 of Shadows of an Empire, Center of the Universe is book 1 of Only the Inevitable, and Optimizing Evil is book 1 of A More Efficient Fantasy. NERiggs.com

First City Books

Anthologies
Romance
Fantasy
Science Fiction

FirstCityBooks.com

Dick Pic

by Don Stoll

If any part of Bobby Conrad was bigger than his dick it was his opinion of his own intelligence. Dewey Thorne envied Bobby's dick, but thought that one day his high opinion of himself would land him in trouble. Still, he'd never said so since Bobby wouldn't have listened. Dewey sometimes thought Bobby was *all* dick. He knew he could never convince Bobby that there had to be a better nickname for his dick than "James T. Kirk"—"Kirk" for short.

"I get the 'boldly go where no man has gone before' thing," Dewey said after he'd waited for Ruth to refill his coffee cup and leave, making his point because it was the right thing to do even though he didn't expect it would do any good. "But the *Enterprise*'s whole crew does that, not just Kirk."

"Kirk's the leader," Bobby said.

He winked.

"Kirk's the head."

Figuring it was a lost cause, Dewey just sighed and shook his own head.

Bobby had more than once "introduced a young lady to the mystery and glory of sex," as he liked to say, imitating the pompous tone of Mayor Alvin Maxwell giving a July Fourth speech. But Bobby mostly avoided virgins because they tended to be under age and he didn't need that kind of trouble. Or trouble with the law period after nearly beating a man to death over his wife in Louisville. He'd told Dewey he'd only gotten away with it because the little queer was too embarrassed to press charges. So "boldly going where no man has gone before" more likely meant a woman trapped in a bad marriage or a widow. Bobby would say he liked to go after a woman who "hasn't done it in so long that her cherry's grown back."

Ruth had heard too much of the trash that Bobby and

Dewey talked. It was hard not to hear with the other breakfast customers come and gone. Thinking that from trash comes more trash, she turned up the radio. She put on WIBC in Indianapolis, hoping to catch the news. Their little town didn't often come up, so she perked up when the smooth-voiced anchor said the station had a reporter on the way to Green Apples. Bobby and Dewey noticed, too, and Ruth was grateful to the radio for shutting them up. But when she began to understand the terrible thing she was hearing about from that voice that was too smooth, the trash Bobby and Dewey had been talking seemed like a little thing.

"Jim and Molly Wagner dead, Ruth?" Dewey said. "He say that?"

"Murder-suicide, likely," Bobby said. "Goes like that with married couples."

"Don't know why she stayed," Ruth said. "Should of got out a long time ago."

They listened while the smooth voice talked like it had something to say, which it didn't with the reporter not in Green Apples yet.

"Dennis will have his hands full with this," Ruth finally said.

"Barney Fife?" Bobby laughed.

Ruth stared at him.

"Andy Griffith's old deputy."

"I know who Barney Fife is," she said. "And that's not fair."

"What's not fair is that with Dennis investigating we'll never know exactly how Jim and Molly Wagner died."

Ruth stared at him hard.

"Different thing in Green Apples," Bobby said, "is that here the deputy's the smart one."

"Which is news to you?" Ruth said. "That a woman could be smart like Cindy Kane?"

Bobby grinned.

"Ruth, I love women."

"Don't waste your time trying to love Cindy Kane," Ruth said. "Got too much going on for the likes of you."

Bobby yawned.

"So much that I guarantee she hates being Dennis's deputy," he said. "Stomach looks like he swallowed his own head. Which makes sense since that shiny thing on his shoulders has all the brains of a bowling ball."

Ruth decided to stop wasting her time talking to trash. She

had lunch to get ready for.

"He'll mess up finding out what happened to Jim and Molly," Bobby said, "you watch her say that's enough. Six months and she'll say Dumb-ass can have Green Apples, this ole country girl's headed to Indianapolis or Louisville or Cincinnati. Hell, maybe St. Louis. Maybe even Chicago."

"Always been the biggest know-it-all in Green Apples, haven't you, Bobby?" Ruth said.

She looked at Dewey.

"There a state tournament for know-it-alls? Reckon your friend could win."

Dewey thought there was a good chance she was right but didn't want to say anything.

* * *

Sheriff Dennis Mowbray of Green Apples, Indiana, didn't share Bobby Conrad's poor opinion of his qualifications for the job. Even so, if Bobby had said to his face what he thought of his sheriffing abilities and that he had the job instead of Cindy Kane only because Cindy didn't have a dick, Dennis might have had a hard time putting up a stiff argument. The only way Dennis could justify to himself that he had the job and Cindy didn't was to promise he'd do his best and always treat Cindy right, remembering that if he'd stepped aside to let her take the job when it was offered everyone would have called him a pussy.

But Dennis wasn't thinking about this when he went with Cindy to Jim and Molly Wagner's place a few miles outside town to investigate their deaths. He only thought he shouldn't assume murder-suicide even though Jim Wagner had been a miserable SOB, and getting worse. A couple of younger mechanics had set up shop who didn't charge more than Jim and were a damn sight friendlier. Jim would ask anybody who'd listen whatever happened to loyalty. But his formerly loyal customers would ask themselves how much they were supposed to put up with when they only wanted their cars fixed, not to listen to Jim explain why the world had gone to hell.

So it's no surprise that Ruth at the diner wasn't the only person in Green Apples to say poor Molly should have gotten out long ago upon hearing that the Wagners' marriage and lives had ended violently. Didn't take Sherlock Holmes to figure this one out, though it was still on Dennis Mowbray and that sharp, pretty deputy of his, Cindy Kane, to find evidence to support the conclusion that just about everyone in Green Apples had come to.

"What's it look like to you, Cindy?" Dennis said as they

studied the bodies.

Because he had so much respect for Cindy he thought it would be best if she went first. That way he could shoot down whatever she said instead of the other way around. Unless he liked what she said, in which case he'd say he'd been thinking the same.

"Murder-suicide probably," she said.

Dennis tried not to let too much hunger show when he watched her, but it was harder when she wore her hair down like she had today. She didn't know and didn't seem to care, but that black shine made him wonder if she had Indian in her. Skin was light, but the dark eyes went with her hair.

"Male deceased holding a Cobra .380," Cindy said. "Bullet wound to his forehead, bullet wound to hers, no sign of a struggle. Male deceased known to have exhibited symptoms of anger, possibly of depression."

"Cobra .380. Cheap and popular, lots of them out there. Maybe he picked it up recently because things came to a head for him? Or maybe not. Maybe somebody would know if he'd owned it a while."

"It's his right," Cindy said.

Dennis turned his eyes from the gun to the dead woman.

"What you make of the female deceased being naked?" he said.

She fought not to roll her eyes.

"Folks are often naked in their bedrooms, Dennis."

He didn't notice Cindy's eyes because he'd been looking at Molly Wagner. But so as not to give the impression of looking at her too long, he turned to Cindy.

"Nothing strange about her being naked and him fully clothed?"

"I'm guessing," Cindy said, "that he'd decided what he wanted to do. He came in ready to shoot while she was changing."

She paused.

"If you were going to kill your wife," she said, "is there any reason you'd want her dressed instead of naked?"

Dennis massaged his chin again.

"Out of respect?" he said. "So people like us wouldn't see her naked?"

"Respect for the woman you want dead because she's partly why your life's messed up?"

"We know that? We know he'd put some blame on her?"

"Well," she said, not quite winning the battle to avoid speaking to him as if he were a child, "he killed her, so I'd say there's a pretty good chance."

So murder-suicide unless additional evidence came to light, Dennis thought. Maybe somebody had witnessed something suspicious: a stranger, an unfamiliar car. But not likely out here, with no neighbors close by.

He closed the file a week later.

* * *

Bobby Conrad's prediction about Cindy Kane hotfooting it to the big city after six months was off the mark. She lasted a year after the Wagner murder-suicide, which had nothing to do with her decision to go since she'd been on the same page with Dennis Mowbray. But she had dreams. She settled on St. Louis.

Her decision hit Dennis hard since he'd figured he was getting close. She'd come out of a bad marriage that soured her on the whole idea of relationships, and he understood because he'd also been in a marriage that went south. He thought Cindy was worth being patient for. Though gradually he began to think the patience being asked of him was unreasonable. He'd thought eventually the pressure on the dam inside her would bust, but it never happened.

So those last two weeks after she'd given her notice were rough while he tried to behave better than ever hoping she would decide she'd be a fool to leave a boss like him. And her last afternoon started with him worrying he'd finally lose his temper, but soon realizing it wouldn't happen. Because he felt defeated instead of angry. So by the time Cindy's last hour began, Dennis felt like crawling into a hole.

Which is when the mail arrived, including a letter with the address handwritten and no return address. The others were bills, so Dennis opened it first and emptied the contents onto his desk: a sheet of paper with some typing on it and a dick pic. He took a moment to marvel at the size of the thing before reading what was on the paper:

Sorry your losing your pretty deputy, sheriff, but you're a loser like Jim Wagner. Was going to do his wife. See the picture, can you blame her? But he came home and said he'd kill me. Went for his Cobra in the dresser but shot him first. Shot Molly too cuz she was a witness and didn't know what she'd say. Felt bad but she was unhappy married to that loser.

Cindy had been in the john. She came over to Dennis when she saw the mail. She picked up the dick pic.

"What you doing with a picture of Bobby Conrad's dick, Dennis?"

93

Dennis looked up from the note. Cindy had turned red like a tomato.

"How you know about Bobby Conrad's dick?"

"It was only once," she stammered. "I was lonely and out having a drink by myself and… well, guess I'd had more than one."

Dennis leaned back in his chair. He folded his hands over his belly. He'd dropped a few pounds trying to look better for Cindy, but still had a good ways to go. And now what was the point?

"Sorry," Cindy said quietly. "Anyway, why you have that picture?"

"Came with Bobby's confession to killing Jim and Molly Wagner."

Quietly, Cindy read the note Dennis handed her.

"No signature," she said. "Except the picture."

Dennis massaged his chin. Always best if Cindy talked first.

"But I'd be reluctant to testify that I recognize his dick. He'd say it was a joke anyway."

"A joke," Dennis said. "How's it a joke?"

Cindy lowered her voice even more.

"Think this is more about you than Jim and Molly. Could be evidence, so he knew you'd have to show me. His way of saying that he. . . you know, with me, but you never did."

Dennis looked at his hands.

"Can see him killing them," Cindy said. "Mean bastard. But when he says this is a joke, and…"

"And?"

"What kind of physical evidence could we collect after a year?"

She'd said it all. Dennis felt defeated every which way.

TO THE BONE, HORLA, YELLOW MAMA, DARK DOSSIER (three times), THE HELIX, SARASVATI, ECLECTICA, EROTIC REVIEW, CLITERATURE, DOWN IN THE DIRT, and CHILDREN, CHURCHES AND DADDIES.

95

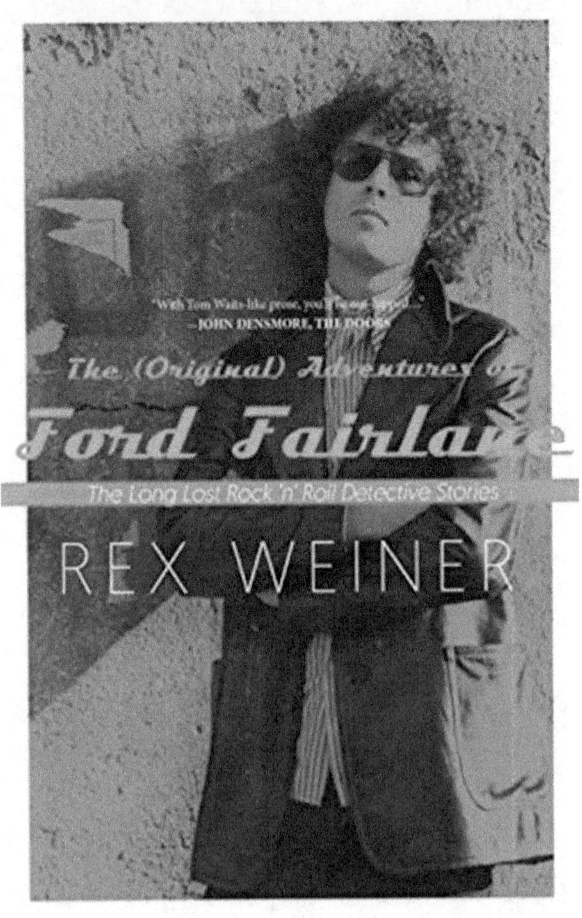

"With Tom Waits like prose, you'll be out-hipped."
- John Densmore, *The Doors*

The (Original) Adventures of Ford Fairlane

RareBirdBooks.com

TOUGH

A journal of crime fiction and occasional reviews
97

www.toughcrime.com

Hoosier NOIR